THE CONTAMINATED 2

This is Getting Rough

CONTENTS

CHAPTER 1

I'm alone now. My body is cold. Its core is a chilled temperature of fucking freezing. This is a brutal winter, no doubt due to my lack of access to electricity. Starting a fire could be the worst decision I've ever made, but when I'm feeling very daring, I'll light one for a few hours. A body's got to stay warm somehow.

Fortunately, food is relatively common in these areas. A lack of people help with that. Everything is preserved in a nice sheet of ice as well. Thawing my food can be a problem, and it doesn't taste quite the same when uncooked, but I need to eat.

Much of what I'm doing now is moving from place to place, town to town. I'm on the run as well as trying to find food for me to eat. The only thing about that is the shit-snacks hunting me down. I'm fleeing as well as searching. It's rough to be honest. I'd say I'm pretty tough for making it this far though - nobody else will, mainly because nobody who can form coherent sentences is alive in these parts anymore.

If I had to guestimate, I'm roaming somewhere near Milwaukee. Then I think of how God has forsaken the northern United States to the devil, but the devil found it too shitty to bother with so the whole thing just froze into one poorly made snow cone.

Let me tell you: snow is bullshit. I can barely move silently through any of these towns or abandoned cities. If I had anyone but you to talk to, I'd be nicknamed captain crunch with every step my boots took. My boots though - the one nice thing about humanity going to shit is that I get my choice of quality boots. These things are really nice, waterproof - camo- the whole shebang and I didn't have to work my ass off getting paid minimum wage to get them either. #perksofbeingalone.

A pack of the contaminated were following me. I was able to circle around them every now and again as they were not very talented trackers. I wasn't either, but these guys were too easy to follow. Of course, if they caught wind of me I fled faster than a tuna at an orca whale convention. Stupid tuna.

The pack of mindless morons was about seven strong. None of them seemed to be the alpha, merely just a set of wanderers looking for the easiest meal they could come across. Other than themselves, that left me. Everything needed sustenance, and since the entirety of the United States population had become nothing more than one large city of a couple million people living behind large walls guarded by bullets which would split a classic 1800's locomotive in half, these guys were very hungry.

There was nothing more that I wanted to do than jump them from behind but that would be loud. Being a noisy individual did not get a person very far in this hostile world. I could probably take them down, the hungry and barely mobile pack of seven contaminated, but that would lead to shouting and roaring, maybe even a gunshot or two if I was sloppy.

While the hunting party wasn't a very intelligent bunch, I had suspicions that the greater contaminated were using them as bait to draw me out. This group was slow, but there are much stronger, faster contaminated which could take me down alone faster than I'd like to think.

My only advantage was the very snow I scrutinized. The contaminated worked off of superheated bodies. They burned energy faster than the flash's metabolism. The cold certainly slowed their ability to function at their normally high rate of movement and aggressiveness. The contaminated were forced to slow themselves otherwise they would burn away so much energy they'd literally eat away at themselves.   Whether my theory was correct or not didn't matter to me as long as I was safe enough. You see, I'm presumably immune to the infection, but my body is not immune to being ripped to pieces - unfortunately.

Maybe that'll be my next immunization trip to the doctors.

I'm feeling risky today though - a sort of adventurous mood which I haven't felt in a very long time. I am finally ready to take down that pack of hunting contaminated. I'm not going to do it all at once, though. As I have previously said a few paragraphs prior, that would be a bad idea. No - I need to do a quick hit and run. I may be able to take out one or two before the rest can react, and by that time I'll be either hidden or long gone.

I had my targets in sight. My pearch, a thick evergreen branch riddled with dark green bristly needles, concealed my body from the slow moving hoard below. The group moved as if they were snails, slogging through the white mess below. The snow wasn't even very high today. Other than a few snowdrifts, there was barely more than four inches on the ground. The contaminated moved right through my field of vision. Their bodies a bright red from the beating cold with thick navy veins breaking the contrast of their skin. There were five women and two men amongst the contaminated, each wearing rags of their former self. Two of the women had jeans on which held against the elements while the others must have had dresses as they were now essentially long rags. Their upper body was merely clad in tank tops, dark spots with mold stains riddling the clothing. The men, or former men, looked as if they forgot to wear clothes the day which they turned into the heated killers. Both looked like former frat boys in nothing but boxers which looked like they might slide off if these guys went without food any longer.

My machete was already unsheathed, its blade solidified cold steel gleaming through the pines. I had a 9mm Glock 17 pistol in my back pocket, but that was only there if things got really dicey. If I had to use my gun, I'd have bigger problems than I could handle. This whole plan was moot if I didn't get a bit of luck anyway.

The seven walked past my position, each in a single file line. It was exactly how I had seen them previously and how I'd hope they would be. Three of the women contaminated lingered at the rear. It was more than I wanted, but maybe it was a sign of luck.

I found my chance. I leapt from my hiding place and crashed into the middle contaminated with the force of gravity behind my machete. It sliced clean along her spine, severing numerous vertebrae. Blood spewed from the rapidly dying woman and onto the contaminated behind me. I did a quick spin and hamstrung the monster and had the machete slicing into its spine before it had a chance to cry out. Two silent kills. The third was right in front of me. She had not noticed the carnage I left behind, and I was feeling greedy for more.

I lashed forward - a cry of rage nearly escaped my lips as I lunged forward. My body twisted at the hips, whipping the blade with even greater force at my foe. The weapon cut true, a clean slice from shoulder to hip. The contaminated fell with little more than the sound of compressed snow.

The remaining four kept walking at their sluggish pace, slogging through the snow. Small clouds of frozen dust kicked up every time one of the monsters' bare foot moved.

Suddenly a roar erupted from behind me. It sounded like a large oak tree being forcefully thrust into a meat grinder, and it made me jump three feet in the air, my sudden movements crashing my head into a low lying branch. After the stars cleared from my view, I realized greed was about to slap me along my head.

Another massive roar erupted from behind the fifty foot tall evergreen I was hiding in. A blur whipped out and crashed into the tree, splitting it in half as if it was a big-ass icicle. The tree crashed to the ground in a flurry of pine needles and powdered snow clouds as my foe revealed itself.

It was a massive contaminated, one who had eaten well during its lifetime. That's how they got so big. It wasn't like humans or normal animals - no - the contaminated could become hulking beasts with massive strength. The one before me stood twenty-five feet tall at least. Its flesh wasn't the normal red-grey of the contaminated. A body this size could release heat fast enough to look like somewhat normal human flesh, with a darker shade of death in it. The colossal contaminated's hands were almost entirely calloused, essentially rocks which could crush a human without a thought. Its shoulders were spread wide, nearly half as long as the body was. Down the length of the abnormally elongated arms was a light coat of red fur, no doubt to contain some of the heat released by the hulking body. The mammoth colossus's head was dwarfed by the rest of its body, the only thing which seemed to be disproportionate. Still, it was about three times the size of the average human's head but was equipped with two six-inch long upper fangs grown to impale into the spinal column of anything living.

Four shots rang out and three contaminated fell. My former entourage was nearly taken down by my pistol before they knew what was going on. I somehow managed to get to my feet and rushed the last one, machete whirling through the air like a ribbon caught in a summer breeze. The final contaminated crashed into the snow. As its body landed, I felt the earth shake and was nearly thrown off balance. The mammoth contaminated took a step - a step which would have woken up a sleeping man.

The monstrosity lurched forward. Each step quaked the earth. Trees lost the snow harboring on their branches and any wildlife in the area fled with cries of fear. I was one of these animals. My feet moved in my quality boots faster than they had to in quite some time. I've been the hunter for these past six months; being hunted made me feel vulnerable.

The mammoth contaminated was fast, but I somehow managed to remain out of its reach. I ran down a main street. It was four lanes wide, at least it looked that way with all of the powdery snow covering the asphalt. I blew through a stop sign and pushed myself down a smaller side street.

It was a residential area. Two story houses lined each side of this WASP street. The lawns were covered in a sheet of white with spokes of dead grass poking through. The sidewalk was not shoveled, forcing me to hop the curb and trespass onto someone's property. I doubt they'd complain.

The monster contaminated was hot on my trail through the

snow mixed with asphalt surely slowed it down so that it could catch its footing. I needed somewhere to go, somewhere contained that the giant couldn't. Slaying the beast was an option, but the resources I would need were a bigger gun, explosives, or both. I had unfortunately run out of my large and dangerous weapons some time back. No - I needed to lose it, to escape its field of view and get away.

I found my ticket to freedom right ahead of me. I turned past a townhouse and hopped over a chain fence before entering a massive open parking lot. A few cars were still scattered about, needless to say none worked but that was not my escape plan anyway.

Directly ahead was the entrance to a mall, aptly titled 'MA-L' with the first 'L' missing due to some big loser hitting it down. My lungs were screaming at me as I bolted towards the broken glass of the double front doors. My legs were beginning to turn numb at the lack of useful oxygen filling them. Cold wind lashed against my face as I booked it across the parking lot. This was my last burst of energy. If for some reason my plan failed, I was going to collapse from exhaustion without a doubt.

The doors were right in front of me. My legs were pushing harder and harder, but the mammoth contaminated was as well. The thundering boom of his massive steps lumbering with such haste pushed me forward even harder. The massive half crescent doors were finally upon me. The glass shattered no doubt from looters and vandals.

I leapt and curled my body into a ball as I passed the open threshold. Hanging glass sliced into my jacket leaving a clean cut through and tearing away some of my flesh. I lost my footing when landing and slid onto my back. My body swiveled with enough time to see the mammoth contaminated crash into the doors. They didn't budge. Its hands were flailing through the opening as it was constantly reaching out to grab me, but unless the contaminated used those hands to pry away the doors, I was safe - for now.

I trudged my way frightened into the dark shadowy mall.

Light reached through the ceiling windows, but that was all. I had no idea what dangers this mall held for me, but in the deep dark of MA-L, I was sure to find out.

CHAPTER 2 - A FOREIGN RITUAL

I'd been in abandoned buildings before, but this mall took the cake for being the creepiest out of any. There were shadows inside of shadows, retching hands reaching out to come drain the life from me. Each corner I turned was blind. Pro tip kids: always check your corners, or send some poor soul ahead to scout for you.

Mannequins lined the halls, arms bending in awkward directions. Most of them were completely naked with missing limbs. One was a male mannequin dressed in a purple blouse and matching plaid mini-skirt. I wondered who the bored soul was that dressed the plastic figurine as such.

There was no doubt that MA-L was once a haven for refugees. The signs were littered about the tiled flooring. Blankets were strewn about, some hanging from wires to create a makeshift tent. Empty cans of food were scattered about these blanket infested areas. Old clothes hung from whatever would hold them to dry, though MA-L was so cold inside that anything liquid was probably frozen solid. Dark sparks of light breached the broken skylights, the ones intact had a sheet of snow and ice atop them filtering out the sun's rays.

I was walking through the main hallway, a mistake by rights as I was completely exposed to the view of any contaminated hiding in the shadows; but the risk was necessary as I needed to scout. There could be valuable supplies in here.

There were three long wings to the shopping complex, each branching off of the main entrance currently cuddling with a massive murderous monster hell bent on ripping my appendages from their places of comfort. Each wing was approximately the same length, each beginning with a massive department store leading into the wings of smaller shops.

I was down the hallway immediately to the left, walking through a large clothing store. It was exceedingly dark in there. No lights came from above as a drop down ceiling blocked anything above. It would be pretty fantastic if there was electricity in this building, somehow preserved over the course of time. I had suspicions that there could be a generator somewhere inside, probably multiple: one for each wing. Unless I found a sign specifically eluding to a power room, I was hesitant to explore the dark reaches of MA-L.

I walked slowly. It was hard to see even an arm's reach in front of me. The only visible sign of light was at the end of the department store, but that was currently being blocked from my view by an escalator. My pace quickened as I wanted to return to that lingering light, my feet stayed quiet in the boots. They were nice boots. A quality bottom grip enabled me to step surely but with a minimal click of boot hitting tile flooring.

I was pretty confident that I could get through this ordeal without making a sound, that was until my stupid fucking boots smashed into a rotating watch display, knocking it over and sending it into the tile with an echoing crash scattering glass and over-priced watches all over the floor in thunderous applause.

A retching scream came from behind me, somewhere near the entrance followed by the mammoth contaminated's roar. Twisted metal yelled in agony at the dark of MA-L as the doorway was ripped from its hinges and loudly tossed into the recesses of the entranceway forum. I'll have to get him on breaking and entering.

I began to flee the scene of the crime. Each step I took seemed to reverberate through the halls of the shopping complex. These stupid boots were giving away my position with every step. I ducked around a dark corner which clipped my left shoulder causing me to stumble down the passageway without will. I followed it, keeping my hand sliding against the left wall so as to not lose myself.

I face planted into a door directly in the darkness before me. My hand groped around for a handle like a virgin's first night before I found its sleek metallic edge. The handle twisted forty-five degrees and the door edged open, greeting me with a creepy smile. I closed the door as quietly as I could, not even the click of the door handle returning to its place sounded, though the screeching hinges gave me a fright.

I decided I could risk a bit more light. I pulled out a mini-flashlight from my back pocket. I clicked the rubber on button on the butt of the light and was engulfed by the LED illumination blaring into my eye-sockets. After I recovered from that violent attack on myself, I looked around to become aware of my surroundings. Flashes of blaring white-yellow clouded my view; the light was damn strong. I flashed it about. I was in a concrete room. Each wall was lined with various water stains mixed with 'essence of mold' perfume. Half rusted pipes flanked the walls as did various wiring depicting the colors of the rainbow.

The corridor split into two paths: left and right. I poked my head around the left hand corner and saw nothing. I tossed the light around and saw a train of wiring leading down the right side corridor. I followed it. Wiring always leads somewhere; whether that place it leads is helpful or not is another question.

The rainbow wiring stretched down the length of the cooridor then ducked into an opening in the wall. Unfortunately for myself, that opening was only about two inches in diameter, thus I was regrettably unable to follow. I was going to find what lay at the end of the tunnel though, I'd come this far; there was no real reason to turn back now.

Double doors stood in my way. There was a chain locking the doors in place. From my past experiences, I learned when something is locked, it is locked for a reason. My past self didn't care right now. I pulled out the steel pipe keeping the chain taught and in place. I kept the pipe in my hand just in case something jumped out at me. A contaminated(s) were probably locked in here at one point, but by now they should all have died of starvation or frozen to death. I was pretty confident in my ability to enter this unknown safely.

I wrenched open the doors with my arms, both swiftly grinding against the rusted hinges as I pulled. I flashed the LED light down the dark corridor. It was more of an elongated closet than an actual passageway. A box, maybe ten yards by fifteen yards of solid concrete lay before me. Large pipes filled with complex wiring were bolted to the walls, protruding from every flat surface like a spear piercing the backside of a decrepit shield. They all led to a disgusting, rusted, moldy, metallic object. It was a vertical cylinder poking out of the ground. A steel vent ran from the top of the cylinder, its rust merging together to create one freak-like monstrosity.

"A generator," my voice finally found me. This shit only happens in the movies; I couldn't believe I was lucky enough to chase myself down the exact doorway I needed to go down. Maybe Hollywood was a bit more realistic than I ever expected their talentless writers to be.

I searched around the rusted waste of an object to search for any way to turn it on. Of course, if power was restored to MA-L, the contaminated would know someone was roaming around here, but my boots already gave away that advantage I had. I hated these boots.

My hand reached forward, sliding across the rough exterior of the rusted steel shell. I pulled my hand away and came off with a nice shade of copper red with a nice metallic smell to it.

The LED reflected off of something bright, a shiny object which wasn't rusted to the core. It was an energy box. This was exactly what I needed. It read:

IN CASE OF EMERGENCY, PULL LEVER UNTIL GENERATOR PRE CHARGED. PRESS CHARGE BUTTON THREE TIMES TO PRIME. CRANK LEVER UNTIL GENERATOR IS ACTIVE.

I did as the instructions - well - instructed. I pumped the lever on the side of the box. It was attached to some kind of gear inside of the generator. My hand then found its way to a bright stainless steel exterior with a red button inside of it. I pressed it. Three times the internal spring pushed the cap back at me, three times I showed that bitch up. Finally, my hand returned to the lever, gliding down the shaft as I did my best impression of a prostitute. I pumped the lever once, then another time, then again. Before long I was pumping that thing up and down so fast my hand began to cramp. Suddenly, it exploded - the generator (don't be perverted) - in a burst of grinding gears and digestion of limited gasoline.

Light engulfed the passageway all around me. My eyes strained at the brightness, readjusting to the yellow glow from above. The light didn't illuminate everywhere, though. The generator was only connected to the essentials, to keep the necessities running as long as possible to hold on until power came back to MA-L.

It was then that I realized why this room was locked off. The walls were lined with people, well at least that's how they looked now. Fourteen bodies - by my count - sat against each of the side walls. A sorry picture of rotting, ruined bodies was plastered to my vision. The stains which I thought were made from water were not. Whether these people had been contaminated - i couldn't know, but this seemed too off for them to be. Contaminated were hard enough to control, let alone make them docile enough not to rip out your jugular. No - these people were contained here. Someone led them to believe they'd be safe, but instead locked them inside to suffer and die of starvation as they tried to claw their way out until the nails were ground away along with the edges of their fingers to draw a bloody mural on the concrete.

It was a grotesque sight, one I was sure to relive in my nightmares.

MA-L was powered now, but for how long, I did not know. I needed to find supplies and get rid of the contaminated on my back. Getting rid of the monsters tracking me was overall more important, but there was no way I could pass up a chance like this. The mall had to be packed with supplies, even with looters already having their choice of goods. There were clothing stores, jewelry stores, random food depots, and some fun places with a random assortment of goods, some of which had to be of use. Plus, there was a freezer to the food square. I doubted it had been totally frozen since the contamination started, but some of what was stored had to be decently edible.

I poked my head out of the room into the dimly emergency-lit hallway. It was clear to move ahead. I pulled the machete tied to my back from its sheath, the pang of sharpened steel ever so quietly sliding against the hardened leather case. My stupid boots made a thudding click on the tiled flooring. I had the option, so I went for it. In my backpack I had a light pair of running sneakers. I'd preferred to wear these when I knew I'd have to flee an area and always kept a pair around. I even had baseball cleats for when I was roaming flat, grassy lands. Making a tight cut as a contaminated chases you, then seeing said contaminated slide - snapping leg bones - and rolling like a barrel of flesh and mutated jello, never lost its appeal.

My sneakers made much less noise on the flooring. The souls of the shoe were made of a flexible rubber instead of the hardened one core on my stupid boots. Each step I took made the equivalent sound of a piece of paper flattening against the earth - aka not much. I reached the intersection, and though my intrigue made me want to see where the fork led, contaminated were roaming around inside of MA-L. I had to get what I needed and get out.

My time was limited to the capacity of the generator's fuel intake, though since it was running now, the power must have been manually turned off for the complex for the generator not to have kicked in when the power initially died.

I made it out into the store's center. Clothing surrounded me, hanging from racks in tiny circles I used to hide between as a kid to scare my mother. Ironically, I was in the women's section with wildly colored lingerie pressing against one side, and granny panties rubbing against the other. I shuddered before moving on.

Light came from the end of the department store. It was the entrance to the chains of stores. I scouted it out quickly. There were three shoe stores, a hat store, a lot of women's clothing stores, a couple fragrance places, a starbucks, and an electronics store. I could totally go for a cup of coffee right now.

I pushed forward past the first few stores. I could always scout them for some clothing, but clothing really was not too hard to find in the barren wasteland of nobody existing anymore. Fragrance was more or less useless, though the compressed bottles of body spray could be turned into nice little mortars if properly made.

There was a store with funky purple and green neon lights in the window. I decided to choose that place to go first. The more random a place, the better supplies it could have - sometimes. The first thing I noticed was a spinning rack, currently disregarding its functionality, filled with different lighters. These were the good kind, or so they liked the customer to believe. Priced between thirty and seventy-five dollars, these were the cream of the crop lighters - they would light things on fire. I pressed open the case, for some reason it was unlocked, and grabbed a handful, throwing them into my bag. I was about to close the case when I saw a lighter that said, 'Stercus Accidit.' I smiled, grabbing the lighter for sixty-six dollars. I flicked open the cap and spun the flint wheel creating a flame. I stared for a minute until the fire blared in my eyes, forcing me to see the flame flicker even after I closed the cap, putting it out.

I rushed out of the store before getting caught up with the fancy flashing lights and electronics I wished I could use (I avoided the adult section). I made it out into the hallway. My eyes up and down the quiet corridor in search of any movement. My body was hidden by a statue of a seven foot tall plastic turkey with large anime eyes and holding a drumstick (the instrument) who no doubt scared many a small child back in its heyday.

Though the frozen escalator passageway hid much of the food court area, I could see a flicker of light. It may have been nothing more than a rat or some bird losing its way near The Wok (average Chinese food), but I was taking no chances. I had light here and I planned on taking advantage of that.

I darted forward into a connecting store. It was a jeweler. The store was mostly unlit by the emergency lights, a mere dim red was emitting from the ceiling. The bloody light reflected off of the glass cases filled with assortments of gemstones and fancy metals. "Some worth you are now," I muttered, glancing down at a glass case as I passed.

A double door was hidden by a draping advertisement 'Everything in life sparkles, but our jewelry lights the way of the future - if only that was a life lesson. I ripped down the plastic paper to reveal the doorway. Its seams were beaming with light from the inside of the tech shop. I was just about to pull open the doorway when something glittered in the corner of my eye.

My arm lashed out with the machete leading the way. I cut clean through the air, embarrassing myself to the nothingness surrounding me. I shook my head, *this place is starting to get to me,* I thought.

It was then that I saw a necklace in the case to my side. It was thin, a thin white gold flexible line which crested into a case holding a ruby the size of my pupil. The ruby was wedged inside a 'v' (ha). The gemstone was so bright and refined it seemed to glow on its own.

It was then that my heart sank. The ruby reminded me of Chelsea. I really was not sure what kind of jewelry she liked, if any, but this was a necklace I liked. I knew if I had the chance to give it to her, she would too. My chance at that moment passed once I was bit by the former member of the CRU. There was no way any human encampment would take a person bitten or scarred by a contaminated. The risk was too high.

I shattered the case with the butt of the machete. Good thing the alarm didn't go off as I wouldn't want the cops after me for this. I reached inside and pulled out the necklace, wrapped it once around my hand and stuffed it inside of my pocket. That wasn't good enough though. I didn't want to lose this piece of my past life, though it had no connection whatsoever, it still weighed heavy on my heart. My machete was placed with a quiet clank of steel on the countertop, and I pulled the necklace out of my pocket. My thumb fumbled with the clasp as I wrapped the glittering metal around my neck. I'd keep this until I died - or had the chance to see Chelsea again.

I tried not to dwell on thoughts of my past life. There was no way I could do anything about it. Chelsea was gone from my time, and she was safe too. I was sure Zach found a way to protect her and that they made it to Kansas City to a safe zone. There was no way that I could think otherwise.

The double door opened with a bit of difficulty, both doors finally giving way to my superior strength (ha). My lenky ass pushed past the threshold and into Computer World. The familiar menacing red light poked through to guide my way. The room was very dark, and none of the sample computers were working. I walked behind the counter. If any of the computers were able to run, it'd be the important ones. The only thing they needed was a hard wire access to the internet, then I could almost get somewhere.

I flicked on the seventeen inch monitor with the side button and slapped down the power switch. The PC was filled with life. Lights on the side of the tower erupted with green and yellow color as the fan erupted in movement in an effort to cool what had been pretty damn cold. I went to the other two computers to the side and turned them on. I knew it was a waste of precious energy, but I couldn't delay. If one of the computers was broken, I needed the others up and running - at least one.

The first computer finally booted on. A login screen appeared, "Shit," I muttered. There had to be something nearby to help with this issue. I flicked through the random papers scattered about the computer. Sticky notes flew through the air (I crushed the hot pink ones. What professional really writes in hot pink? Even if it is your shitty retail job sucking the remaining life out of your already lifeless, energy deprived, customer abused body, you can still write on a goddamn yellow sticky note. You're not a fifteen year old high school bitch [unless you are(and bitch is gender neutral; don't start with me on that)] so don't act like one) as I rummaged around the desk.

"Finally!" I said louder than I should have. I ripped out a neon green (don't) sticky note which read: PC101. I plugged the obnoxiously colored note into the password section and slammed my pinky finger down on 'enter' as hard as I could for a nice dramatic effect.

The password went through and the bright blue desktop slowly loaded into effect. I quickly checked the corner of the workbar and saw that the internet was flowing freely. Score. The screen was touch enabled so I obnoxiously tapped the internet browser, littering the once shiny and smooth surface with an assortment of blotchy fingerprints. I went to the only place I could think up.

The Last Uncontaminated Forum loaded into view. I was glad the website was still up and running. It never occured to me that someone must be doing it off to the side without us knowing. The admin must have had the server somewhere safe with electricity. My guess was Kansas City, but I probably would never know for -

ZmB1EtR: YOU'RE ALIVE!!

DR. YlSRUS3390: Somehow I am.

ZmB1Etr: Good to hear from you. How've things been?

DR. YLSRUS3390: No time to explain. I'm in a mall somewhere in Milwaukee. Got no idea where I really am. Something is in this place with me.

ZmB1Etr: Sounds rough. Hang on

ZmB1EtR: ...

ZmB1EtR: Got it! I found you.

DR. YLSRUS3390: Great. How does that help me?

ZmB1EtR: Come to me. I'm in Denver, you know that

DR. YLSRUS3390: I'm hesitant. Last time I trusted someone on here they tried to kill me.

ZmB1EtR: Who was that?

DR. YLSRUS3390: No time dude. Where's the nearest power zone to here?

ZmB1EtR: Kansas City, though you'd be there by now. Other than that you'd have to come to Denver.

DR. YLSRUS3390: ...

ZmB1EtR: Just come. You and Chelsea will have enough room here to hunker down for a bit.

DR. YLSRUS3390: Just me.

DR. YLSRUS3390: Where?

ZmB1EtR: Sorry. According to my maps, if you had a car you could get here in a day if you pushed it. By foot, that would take a bit longer. Just come to Denver. I'll find you.

DR. YLSRUS3390: Hesitant about giving information to me?

ZmB1EtR: You don't trust me either. So we're even by that right.

DR. YLSRUS3390: At least would you finally give me your name?

ZmB1EtR: When you get here.

DR. YLSRUS3390: C'mon, be a bro!

ZmB1EtR: Can't, sorry.

A crash echoed from inside the department store off to my side. Someone or something was rummaging through the insides of a clothing rack. I doubted it was a contaminated, but maybe they just started this whole plague to improve their sense of style.

DR. YLSRUS3390: Sry gotta go. Bad shit is around. I'll find you in Denver.

There was no time to wait for a response. I ripped the power cords from each of the powered devices (terrible shutdown etiquette). Life immediately drained from the computers as they all went blank. I ducked behind the counter. My pistol had three shots left in the magazine. There was more ammo in my pack, but I had no time to load it.

I crept along the edge of the store, sure to keep my body down. I had to get out of here now. My foolish lingering took too long resulting in my enemy getting close. There had to be some good things in here, but I had no choice but to leave now. My mission changed from just surviving to thriving. Denver would allow me to live like a person again. I had to have a little trust placed in ZmB1EtR, even if they couldn't put it in me (ha).

Another crash followed by an angry scream. I couldn't tell what kind of contaminated it was, though if it was still screaming instead of loosing a bellowing roar, it was probably freshly turned. Some poor sucker probably survived in this wilderness for months - eluding the contaminated with every ounce of strength in their body only to succumb to the inevitable eventually.

"Nothing good in here," The voice hissed. It was feminine with a hint of raspy clogged voicebox. Something your mother used to grind against a rock to sharpen in her dinosaur days. "This shit won't fit."

"You've only got like three more days anyway," another smug voice called from behind. "What's it matter what you wear?

You're going to turn sooner than later."

"I want to look nice as I turn. So many of our brothers turn and ruin their clothes into rags. I want something durable that will last," the voice of one thousand dying zebras lashed back.

"Whatever," the smug man/woman/squirrel said. "Do you think the person who turned on the generator is still in here? Maybe one of our brothers got to him."

Plastic hangers clattered against the tiled floor as questionable person A couldn't decide on their dinnerware. "He looked crafty - a quick little shitter he was. Probably still in here if he was smart."

"I'm turning the generator off," questionable person B said. "No reason to have it on. It'll impede our brother's pilgrimage."

"Whatever you wish, but I'm finding something decent here. Don't worry about the lights, my eyes are already evolving to be like those of our brothers and sisters. Before you go, what do you think of this neon pink suit? A bit gaudy, but I'd look so hot."

I could hear person B rolling their eyes, "What professional wears a hot pink suit?"

Person A scoffed, "Who said anything about professional? Besides, I'll be a rookie compared to some of our other siblings."

"A rookie, maybe. But you've been at three group bleedings so far. You know what you're getting yourself into."

"Mm-hm," freak A replied. "I can't wait until you have your first blood. It's such an invigorating rush. We are making history here, my future brother. What the remaining freaks call the 'contamination' will be remembered by our brethren and the lords above who bestowed this blessing upon us."

There was an awkward silence, so awkward I even felt like breaking it up. Finally, weird-ass-creep B spoke, "I'm sorry, I don't think there is a good shot at me getting my first blood. The lords did not grace me with maidenhood."

"You're such a shit sometimes," raspy-shitmouthed-sockwad (sorry ran out of ideas for that last bit) said. "Go turn off that damn generator. It'll distract more of our siblings and bring them our way, that is, unless you'd rather your first blood be here.

Just be careful, they may be hungry-"

"I'm going," person B-itch (ugh) replied.

The rusty hinges to the maintenance door screamed down the passageway. Once I heard them come to a close, I pushed out from my hiding spot. The machete was clasped in my left hand, the 9mm tightly gripped in my dominant right. I slowly closed on the sound of clothes racks being searched and hangers being blasted from their hooks onto the sleeping floor.

I brushed aside a circular section of clothing - large, heavy winter coats - and crept inside. It was like a miniature fort, not quite as exciting as I remembered from childhood, but still cool nonetheless. It brought back memories of when I used to hide inside of these while my mom frantically searched the sections for her lost child. Once found, I was taught never to do that again - firmly.

I could only see the person's feet reflecting their shadow onto the floor, everything else was far too dark for my eyes. The hot pink and navy blue sneakers were hastily moving across the room, rack to rack, in search of the ultimate clothing find. I was three sales away from the random individual.

There was no other choice. My move was swift and graceless. I tumbled out of the clothing rack, a hanger hook catching me around the collar before snapping. I performed a jig with the solid floor before my feet found themselves and pushed me upwards. I had the exit side of the pistol aimed at the person's head with the machete under the nose of the weapon to steady it.

"Who're you?" person A asked.

I swallowed hard, "That's none of your business," my voice was shakier than it should have been. "What are you doing here? What is this business about a pilgrimage and - brothers? Your buddy isn't here so you better start talking before he returns. I'm not going to be talking to two at once if you understand my meaning." I'd never shot at a person before, a living human anyway. I really did not want to either. There were so few remaining humans left in the world, it seemed really stupid for a human to kill another. "Answer fast or I will cut you!" I said with a near raised voice. This person's partner was not too far away, I only hoped he/she couldn't hear me.

Person A took a slow step forward, her arms stretched out wide as to not raise an alarm, "There's no reason for the violence, friend. We are all part of the lords' creation and demise. You are a brother as well as me and my friend along with the millions of us fighting against oppression. The lords blessed us with a gift greater than any other - to evolve. Do you not see it too?"

"None of that answers my questions. One last chance. Next thing you speak better mean something."

She took a wide - red smile, "But everything i say does matter. It is the answer to your questions." The woman took another step towards me. She was two short paces away now. "If you would just let me show you - GAH!" The woman roared as I did a quick spin and lashed the machete into the back of her upper thigh, hamstringing the woman. She fell to the ground in a heap of pain and anger. "Once I evolve - oh once I evolve, you will be my first blessing!"

"What does that even mean?" I asked before receiving a blunt object smash against the back of my head.

It hurt. My head throbbed - wibbly wobbly. I couldn't move my arms at all. My legs were resting against the ground. I was sitting now. How did I get to be seated? I don't remember sitting - or tying my hands behind my back. I wasn't into that kind of stuff. Right?

My skull felt as if it was trying to keep the beat of a drum for some god forsaken high school band at their first show. There was a sudden cold hand gripping me under the chin and across my jaw. "You will be her first blessing," the voice of person B said. I opened my eyes to see what I believed to be a young man standing above me. He had a dark fluffy winter jacket on with a lining of fur around the hood. A small fire was lighting the darkness in his eyes.

"Whas a firs blessn'?'" I asked through clenched cheeks.

He loosed his hand grip from my face and circled the fire, "The first meal. You will be her first meal - to nourish and grow. That's a blessing if I ever heard one. The lords are good to her due to her undying loyalty. She knows that she will be blessed with evolution soon enough."

"Does she have a name?" I asked out of curiosity.

"Not for you."

"Well my machete has a name, Chetty, and I'm sure she misses me a lot. Mind returning her, preferably to my right hand?" I had to ask.

It almost looked like the boy smiled, "Sorry, can't do. Chetty is close, but you won't have any time to say your last good-byes. She'll be awake any minute now. So I have to run, but this was a nice chat."

"Wait!" I tried to sound desperate. "What is your name at least?"

He looked as if he was hesitant to tell me. I could tell by the way his large frame started back and forth with indecision. "Marvin."

"Nice to meet you, Marvin."

"I'll almost regret not talking to you longer. You seem like a personable-"

"My nine-mil is named Milly. I'm sure she'd love to talk to you. She's a bit loud, but you get the point."

Without a word, Marvin turned and walked away into the darkness.

There wasn't much left to do. I tugged on my ties with a loose effort. The ropes burned into my wrists making them feel almost like fish wire. My head darted left and right, but the fire wasn't bright enough to reveal anything to my sides. It was only there so that I could see the horror approach me.

She stirred, a subtle twitch. Her hands clenched then relaxed then clenched again. Someone was ready for their blessing.

I needed to get out, now. There had to be some way to set me free from these bindings. I turned and tugged at the ropes with all of my might as my assailant slowly began creeping forward. She was on all fours, or threes as her back leg was limp from when I cut it. There was a scrape of steel on cement. Marvin must have left the machete and Milly behind this fresh blood thinking it was safe.

I rolled and writhed in desperation now. There was nothing else I could do until I felt something sharp jab into the side of my leg. *The lighter!* I hooked my hips as close to the pole holding my hands in place. I pressed hard against the ropes, just far enough to where my fingers could wiggle into the seam of my jean pockets. They fumbled for the cap, eventually pulling it open. I did not need this thing lit inside of my pants. That was not how I wanted to go.

The woman stirred again, her face was close to the fire now. She had dark yellow eyes and pale flesh. Her hair looked normal and she was wearing a hot pink suit torn at the side of the skirt to reveal way too much leg. Let me tell you, there is no such thing as a sexy contaminated.

My thumb finally wrapped around the lighter and brought it back. Another limp forward. It flicked the flint wheel, sending a wave of heat up my arm. A stumbling limp forward. *She's getting too close.* There was no time to prepare myself. *Too damn close.* I pressed the flame against my left hand bindings. Heat roared through my wrists as flesh slowly melted away from the bone, but so did my bindings. I tore my left arm free and my right quickly followed. I was in immense pain, but there was still danger afoot.

She was too close for her own comfort now, and I think she knew it. The bitch looked up in fear as my shoe collided down on her head, crashing it into the ground. I stomped again, this time farther down to the neck. A distinct crack sounded from inside the woman as I nearly severed her spine. My good boots would have done it in one go. I looked around and found the machete. My right hand picked it up. I looked at the pathetic slob laying on the ground, breathing heavily as she no doubt knew her life was coming to an end. *This is no evolution* I thought as I brought the blade down upon her neck. She stopped moving instantly. "Shit happens," I muttered.

I knew what I had to do now. There was no other direction for me. I'd fix my hand first, then - I was headed to Colorado.

CHAPTER 3 - CHELSEA

"Ahhhh!" I released the inner tension in the back of my throat through a yawn. Dawn just sprung over the window, it's orange-yellow hue blasting its way into my sleeping quarters. I stretched my arms, wringing them out along the soft egyptian cotton sheets lining one of the last tempurpedic mattresses in existence. I was sleeping on what is now a collectors item since none were being produced since the contamination took place.

A feeling of dread washed over me all of the sudden. It was hard being in a completely different place. My life had been a turnstile weaving rapidly in the wind for the past few months. Nothing seemed to sense anymore. It was mostly a lifestyle of: what will get me through today and into the next. It made me miss my old life quite a bit, especially the internet. I could have spent hours online at a time doing literally nothing at all other than staring at the blue light of my computer monitor, but it made me happy. That was probably the only thing I really enjoyed about the contamination - the removal of society's absurd standards of normalcy. Nobody cared anymore what exactly I did. It was none of their business and that's how it should have always been. If the contamination ended, I'd almost be disappointed - almost.

It was comfortable here, in this bed. I was warm and totally not ready to take on the day. There was so much work to be done, as if my life's journey was never going to be at an end. I know I'm pretty young to be complaining about this but that's how it is.

How did the contaminated live? It was a question to which I pondered many a moon. They were clearly intelligent - not enough to operate machinery and problem solve (for the most part), so what did they think their lives were? Are we, as humans who kill contaminated on sight, responsible for the genocide of a different race? But at the same time the contaminated try to kill humans and destroy them for their own gain. The only difference is that humans kill to survive while contaminated kill to live. I think too much, sometimes.

The sun was warm today. It was about time. The past few days have been a frigid freezing ferocious frost land. A bit of heat in the sky was just what was needed for today.

A shadow suddenly blockaded a portion of the sunlit window. A short-haired black cat with white paws and a bleached nose was basking on the windowsill enjoying the heat. I shook my head, "Coal, I was enjoying that too," I said. She replied with a heavy purr and a flick of her long tail.

My door opened at the same time. "Morning," Chelsea said nonchalantly. She began pulling off the comforter, causing a wave of cold rushing over my body. "We need to get moving today, you know that. It's one of our first days with an assignment."

I wrapped the down pillow around my face in a poor effort to have it suffocate me and relieve me of my duties for the day. "Don't remind me," I replied through muffled pillow. "They're giving me the hard and scary job. I'm kinda claustrophobic ya know."

"No you're not," Chelsea replied as she yanked the pillow away from me. "Come on, Zach."

I caved into her outrageous demands and pulled myself out of bed. I don't know what she was fussing about. I get dressed in a matter of minutes - which I did - and am ready to be out the door. It was now my turn to wait by my apartment exit for Chelsea to come running down the stairs, claiming she forgot to wear her running shoes and accidently slipped on boat shoes (really? boat shoes in the face of the apocalypse? Some god somewhere must have been laughing at that one). "Ready, princess?" I muttered bravely as she *finally* approached.

I really could not figure out what took her so long. The apartment was only one bedroom, one bathroom, and a depressingly small kitchen merged with a room titled the 'living room' though there wasn't much living to be had there. A red and green Christmas themed couch lined one wall as the piece of furniture and a severely underfilled bookshelf placed along the other. The only nice thing about the room was the large half crescent window overlooking the entirety of Kansas City and the wilderness beyond.

"Okay, let's go," Chelsea said as she finally appeared at the bottom of the stairs. I was already set on the sidewalk waiting to go. "What do you think?" she asked with a twirl ending as she strutted out her hips. Chelsea had a light leather jacket on with zipper pockets right above the breast. Tight camo leggings lined her lower half ending with a set of standard hiking boots. The hood of the jacket was pulled over her deep chestnut hair. Dark aviator sunglasses hid her ocean blue eyes. And her curving slender hips were covered in hips with hips and when she turned there were camo hips right by the hips which had even more - "Okay stop staring," she said.

"You look marvelous," I replied, suddenly conscious of what hopefully wasn't protruding inside of my jeans. I only wore a flannel white long sleeved shirt. It was chilly outside this morning, but I was going to be doing hard physical labor. I'd even opted for sneakers even though boots would probably be better for the condition of my toes - but if I was caught out in a dead race, I'd probably at least not lose.

We made our way down the non-busy streets of Kansas City towards the edges of the city. It didn't take too long as the apartment was pretty close to the city limits. The once over crowded streets were closer to a barren wasteland now. Drifting papers didn't even flow as the concrete was left lonely and unprotected from the decay of humanity. It was sad to see buildings abandoned and others just simply knocked down for their resources because there was no way to fill them with people.

The only good thing to come of it was the construction of the city gardens. These were once bustling areas of the city which could simply serve no purpose in the modern world. Anything that would use excessive electricity or a gas station which was emptied was simply torn down by manpower. That was really the only thing needed anymore. We didn't have much gas or enough electricity, but what humans did have was time and boredom. They would hustle over by the droves to dig something up or work for extra food cards.

That's another interesting invention of the post-contamination. We rationed food like I never had to before. It wasn't as if anyone was starving though, especially with the addition of the city gardens. But it never felt as if you got your full fill. Nothing was ever used in excess and no food was wasted. You ate what you had or you put it in a fridge and saved it for later, no matter how little it was. One thing Chelsea came up with was everything soup. It was literally everything leftover from the week shoved in a boiling pot of water. She'd sometimes soak the meat in the water to give it a bit of extra flavor, but for the most part - it was always a pleasant surprise.

The city gardens were built and maintained by a labor force strictly confined to the city. The massive gardens were essentially a small farm dedicated to the use of the people. The planters grew and maintained everything they could. Broccoli, lettuce, squash (ugh), and anything else green which could grow. The only unfortunate bit was that it was winter, and not much enjoyed growing in the winter. They did fix up a greenhouse, but its yields were nowhere sufficient for everyone else.

I almost got stuck in the canning facility - a place where one's job was literally to can anything cannable. Preserve the perservable, preserve humanity! - was the slogan of the place. As much as my job may have scared me, there's no way it would be worse than canned goods.

We reached the wall, or what was to be the wall. As of now, it was a fence with actual wall only fortifying the weakest and most blind areas. So it was kind of like an angry fence at this point. The chainlinks rose high though, reaching the point where anyone would be not well greeted by the hard ground if they decided to jump down. There was only one situation of a contaminated trying to climb over. It promptly died.

"Alright, fucks - I mean - folks," the sergeant began. "You know your role today. Though an encounter is of the rare variety, please don't ruin everyone else's experience by screwing this up." The man was in full camo gear from a short brimmed hat to his boots. It was a chilly day outside, but he showed no sign of caring about the lowered temperatures. "We got a job to do, so let's go do it." The man marched over towards the entrance stables.

"Horses smell so bad," I whispered to Chelsea. It was the main form of transportation outside of the walls. It gave for a quieter passage and more immediate access in the wilderness. A horse could navigate through a heavily wooded area while a jeep could not. One wasn't really preferred over the other, it was just for convenience sake.

"Tolerate it, please," she replied as the reins of a brown spotted steed were handed to her. "The last thing we need is to get kicked out because you don't want to ride a horse."

I furrowed my brow, "I really enjoy riding the horses - it's a lot of fun. They just smell is all." The stableman handed me a horse of my own. A black steed with puffy white hooves towered before me. It was really a beautiful horse. How I earned that one, I'll never know. I stuck one of my feet in the hold and lurched myself overtop, landing with a gentle thud on the saddle. Chelsea did the same next to me, a small leather pack slung over her shoulder.

Green and white flags were waiving above the gates of the wall, signaling our clearance to move. In total, about twenty of us were venturing beyond the walls into the wilderness beyond. Twenty steeds began kicking up dust clouds of lingering snowfall as we raced down the main platform. Each step kicked up puffs of dry snow to create golden flickers of the morning sun in clouds.

Before the cold began to numb my hands, we were at the forest's edge. Not too deep into it lay an abandoned coal mine which was still able to produce coal. It was nice in the forest. It seemed as if the air was thicker in here, easier to breathe than the thin dry air of winter. It was also warmer, the trees protecting us from the wind's whipping.

We stopped right at the edge of the trees. Our only issue

with the mission was that we had two larger carts attached to horses. The mission was to mine as much coal as possible and cart it between the mine and the edge of the forest where the carts were waiting for us. We had elongated saddlebags which could hold a decent amount of the rocks, but it wasn't enough to supplement what we really needed.

"Okay hold here," the sergeant said with an eerie kindness in his voice. "Everyone has their quiet weapons and their loud ones. Do not use the loud unless completely necessary. I implore you - and I rarely implore. Guards will only be near the mine save three. The transport carts are armed so we don't need to waste resources there. The three I choose will be the coal transport guard. They will protect the carrying of coal from the mine to the carts for depositing. Understood?"

"Yes!" Everyone in the group said in a clear voice.

This plan worried me. Though it had been executed numerous times before, it left me wondering if it was only by dumb luck. I did the math: two carts with four people on them, three transport guards, and ten miners. That left only three more guards stationed at the mine. On top of that, some of the miners would be S.O.L. if we were attacked. To prevent any delay in production, the guard would lead a riderless horse through the woods. This way it could carry more coal and the miner could keep mining coal.

"There has only been one attack in the short history of this operation!" The sergeant continued louder than I cared for him to be. "Let us keep it that way. Everyone watches out for everyone and we all come home without an issue." A small 'whoop' echoed from the crowd. "You three," the sergeant said, pointing to Chelsea, a short man with a balding scalp induced with numerous scars, and another woman clicking the magazine of her dark barrelled rifle into place. "You will be the escort of the coal-bearing horses. Do you understand your mission?"

Chelsea wouldn't be at the mine. "Yes, sir!" They all replied without hesitation.

"Chels," I said, quickly pulling her to the side. "Be safe."

She winked at me, "We're always safe." Chelsea gave me a nice long kiss. "Just wait until later tonight."

CHAPTER 4 - A NEW JOURNEY

Mining was tough work. My arms ached, my back ached, my legs ached, and even my head ached (though more from having an actual headache than mining). I wasn't even one of the ones doing the swinging of the pickaxe either. I was just transport - the constant slogging back and forth wheeling a barrow to and from the miners. I filled the wheelbarrow then emptied it into the saddlebags on the horses waiting near the edge of the mine. It sucked. My hands were a deep shade of musty black which extended halfway up to my elbows. I was sure to have soot and coal dust on my face from wiping away the sweat from my forehead with the back of my hand, streaking it across my brow.

The mine was about one hundred feet deep, and deepening by the day. The ceiling was none too high, forcing anyone with considerable height to walk with a severe crouch. This process also hurt one's back.

This was a dangerous operation for more than one reason. There was the threat of being attacked by the contaminated, of course, but on top of that there really were no mining experts still alive. We had a few engineers looking into the mine and examining where the weak points may be and how to prevent a collapse, but even they were unsure if what they were fortifying was really the right move. In essence, there was a chance that the coal mine could collapse on us at any given moment.

We needed to do this, though. The only operational power plant lived off of fossil fuels. We had reserves of coal in the actual plant, but that would run out one day. This operation ensured longevity, at least until we could find another way to generate electricity.

There was one more way, but it was more of a work in progress. The very engineers attempting to keep the mines from collapsing onto everyone inside of them were also in the process of building a water powered plant. This plant would also be connected to wind turbines to create an extra form of electricity. It would be the first post-contamination power plant ever created. It was being built slow, though not for lack of knowledge on how to do it, but due to lack of resources. Parts were extremely hard to come by, useful ones anyway, so many had to be made with very little material.

Unfortunately for me, I was stuck doing this work for another hour at least. These operations generally didn't carry on for too long as the danger was too real. Once a cart was full, it left for the city without looking back. Once it reached the city, the drivers abandoned the cart and took two fresh horses to ride back as an escort to the second cart. We'd been at this for almost an hour now. The first cart was bound to be nearly full. After the second cart was filled, the mission was over and we all went back to the city. After the three hour mark, everyone dropped what they were doing and packed up. It was rare that the three hour timeframe was ever hit, but the sergeant would not risk being there any longer than that. The chance that a wandering contaminated could hear some noise and rally its comrades was too high.

I hadn't seen Chelsea in a half an hour, though. It worried me seeing as it was only about a twenty minute slow ride to and from the carts. Even if she helped unload the saddle bags, which the escorts generally didn't, it shouldn't take her this long to get back. She could have just stayed a minute or two just chatting with whoever was with the carted horses, but I didn't think she knew any of them to have an extended conversation with. I was probably concerned for nothing more than my own superstition.

The saddlebags of the horse waiting right outside the cave

were full. I tossed the last dark rock into the bags before closing it, pulling the leather strap tight. The light brown horse tossed its head and shuddered as it shimmied the weight of the bags around.

"This one's ready," I said to the smaller man on a brown horse of his own.

He twisted around in the saddle to inspect the bags. "Seems ready. Nice and tight there. Good work...uh."

"Zach."

He nodded, "Good work, Zach. Name's Matthieu," the balding man said as he rubbed the remaining charcoal colored hair on each side of his head.

"Rub it in," I jested. "The coal will make your hair look younger. It's the only Rogaine left."

Matthieu let out a full laugh from deep within his portly belly. "Not bad, kid. I'll be off then." Matthieu grabbed the reins and pulled the horse towards him. The light brown steed had no interest in moving with any form of haste, merely moving forward with his leader's command.

"Matthieu!" I called after he was a few paces away. The man swiveled in his saddle but didn't stop the horses. "Can you do me a favor and just see if Chelsea is on her way back. I'll probably see her before you can say anything but just keep an eye out for her." Matthieu gave a slight head nod. Before he disappeared into the wood, he drew a long knife from its sheath.

I couldn't help but stare into the woods after Mattieu. It was too quiet today. Even the miners were making little noise. It was as if someone lined their pickaxes with cotton balls to mute them. A light chilling breeze blew, knocking my hair into my face.

"Problem?" It was the sergeant's dangerous voice. I panicked for a moment before realizing I had done nothing wrong.

I played off my fear, pushing it away. I turned to the sergeant with a shrug, "Just wondering where Chelsea has been. It's been a little while. She should have returned with the packhorse by now." I had a little fear in telling the sergeant this. He would tear into me any second now.

"What is this pansy attitude I hear from you boy?" He asked in a tone my heightened voice had no chance at replicating. "She's a good shot. There's no way your girl will not come back. This tardiness is concerning, however. She'll have to do a few laps in the yard if she keeps it up."

His confidence in Chelsea helped shake off my fear. It was true that Chelsea was a good shot and nobody doubted it. There was a tournament a few weeks back, shortly after we arrived here in Kansas City. Chelsea had already learned how to shoot from Daryll to an extent, but she quickly picked it up here as well. With the lessons provided by the sergeant and other military staff, Chelsea rapidly rose the ranks of sharpshooterdom. The tournament had about fifteen entries, including myself. No military personnel were allowed in the tournament. The prize was a nice ration of extra sugar and deep maroon steaks fresh from the slaughterhouse. I wasn't a bad shot either.

"Do you really think you can beat me?" I asked Chelsea. I was shooting my trusty 9mm. It was all that people could use at the tournament seeing as it was the only readily available ammunition.

Chelsea scoffed, "You're not my biggest challenge. This tournament is easy. No targets are moving," she said brushing her autumn hair out of her eyes. There was a light breeze, but it would not have an effect on our rounds.

The last challenge was a do or die set. There was an eight inch pan being held up by a rope. The challenge was to get the best cluster out of four shots. The cluster would be measured by proximity to the bullseye.

"Ladies first," I said with a chivalrous wave of my hand.

Chelsea smiled, "I'm a modernist. Please, you first."

I didn't want to go first. I have always hated going first. I liked to watch the others and play off of what they did, a reactionary type of game. Nonetheless I readied my weapon.

The forks atop the pistol were aligned with little room for error. My finger slipped over the trigger with my left palm steadying the weapon from below. I fired once, then again, then again, and finally my fourth shot. Someone quickly ran over and nabbed the pan from its post, taking it off to the side for measurement. I glanced over as someone was replacing the target. My shots were good, pretty damn good. Confidence was my superior ally.

I was boasting with my chest fully puffed and ready to proclaim victory when Chelsea took her turn. It sounded like a firecracker, her shots going off in a rapid burst. Pop-poppoppop. There was no time to even hear the grazing of the bullet tearing through the aluminum alloy of the pan.

Chelsea didn't even wait for an official word as the entirety of the crowd was stunned by her performance. When someone finally went over to the pan to observe the cluster, they didn't even bother with measurements. I could have beaten her, gotten my shots more accurate to the target, but there was no match in speed. Chelsea was on an entirely different level than I was when it came to sharpshooting.

She went over to the cooler and pulled out the tightly wrapped steaks and grabbed a couple of ration cards as well. "Eating good tonight!" she exclaimed to me. Chelsea was promptly dubbed: The Queen of Calibur.

I asked her later that night how she learned to shoot that well, so aggressively but with such accuracy.

"I'm determined," she merely replied.

"You're right, sir," I said to the sergeant. "There's no way anyone is touching her while she's armed."

The sergeant patted me on the shoulder, "Don't be so hard on yourself. You've got an excellent shot too. If Matthieu didn't have a bad back and Miranda wasn't weak as shit, you'd be on one of those horses no doubt." The sergeant looked around, "Here," he said, handing me a collapsible rifle. "Stick that somewhere safe. It's loaded - I know I know - just be careful with it. If shit goes down, you'll need that more than I."

There was a deep guttural sound, a gurgling of mucus and phlegm against the back of something's throat. I spun around immediately, clicking the compact rifle into place and steadying it in my shoulder. My left hand was sitting under the barrel to steady the weapon. I had a feeling it shot some lower caliber round, but before I knew it, I felt a weight in my right pants pocket. I glanced down to see the sergeant placing a magazine of .556 along with a few extra rounds in my pants. He gave a silent nod and readied a way cooler looking rifle of his own.

Of course, I thought, *right as the sergeant was starting to warm up to me some shit's about to go down.* I had no idea what to do, to be honest. This was my first real encounter fighting the contaminated in the wild. I hope the sound wasn't produced by a contaminated, but it was all too familiar nowadays. No - there was something dangerous and very real ready to strike from the underbrush.

"Wanna trade?" I whispered to the Sergeant jokingly.

He whipped around to the sound of the wind blowing against a dead creaking tree limb. "I do not want to trade. My rifle is my rifle. That rifle is now your rifle," he whispered in reply. "We both know what that sound was. Shoot to kill, don't play with your food."

"What happened to going quiet?" I asked.

I heard the sergeant unsheath his knife, solid steel gliding against leather, "Quite if possible." The sergeant raised his knife perpendicular to the rifle, steadying the weapon with one hand while holding the knife ready to attack with the other. "If it shows itself, I'll go for the silent kill. But use your discretion when covering me. If it looks bad don't hesitate. Hesitation kills people."

It saves them too.

The forest was so quiet when I tried to listen. Nothing stirred in the middle of the desolate winter. A chill ran up my spine with the corresponding breeze no doubt turning my cheeks a rosy red. *Where are you?* I asked myself knowing full well that there would be no answer, at least I hoped not. The last thing humanity needed was for mind reading contaminated.

Suddenly, an ear splitting cry rang out from a horse not too far away. Before I knew what happened, two shadows popped out of the brush covered in snow. They were running hard at us, their upper bodies covered in nothing but their own superheated flesh. Their arms were lashing out against us as if they were trying to swim at us through the air.

POP-POP! Our rifles went off before the contaminated had a chance to get anywhere near us. We couldn't risk the silent kill with multiple assailants. The cry of more contaminated echoed in the distance. "Three more," the sergeant whispered through gritted teeth.

Before I had time to assess my surroundings, the feet pounding against the hardened earth ran towards us. The three contaminated were on us in an instant. POP-POP two fell. "Rawr MOTHERFUCKER!" the sergeant yelled as he lacerated the last contaminated with his massive knife, cutting the monster across its throat then wedging the blade deep into its back. "Had to let off a little steam, you know?" the sergeant asked.

I looked around in search of more contamination. More were shouting and crying out in their rage echoing through the heavy vegetation but none showed themselves.

"Grab the miners, we're getting out of here," the sergeant commanded. I immediately obeyed, not only because I was a good soldier (ha) but because I wanted to get the hell out of here as well. When the action was high and tight, my trigger finger was ready for any endeavor. But when the clam hit before the contaminated did, that was when I began to have thoughts of worry.

I slammed the butt of the rifle against a steel support beam. The metallic sound reverberated through the entirety of the mine. It then occurred to me that I could have caused a cave-in. Oh well.

"What's up," one of the miners asked. He was surrounded by a few others, though some undoubtedly were still dedicated to their posts and remained inside. "We heard a few gunshots."

"A few contaminated attacked. Get everyone ready. We're heading out immediately," I replied.

The lead man - I really should be learning names by now - ran deep into the cave in search of the remaining company.

"Sir," I said, performing my best salute. "Where are the other two guards? We're going to need them here to escort the men without horses."

The sergeant spit into the earth after a hefty hawking, "They're on scouting duty. To be honest with you, I have no idea where they are. My men could be in the trees waiting to strike or on horses already fleeing. Hell, they could be dead for all I know. Those contaminated got through somehow, and if I was a betting man, which I am not, then my money would be on those two not being alive anymore. They were sharpshooters, similar to the ability of myself-" the sergeant cut his words with a grunt. His eyes became wide, staring into the distance of the woods. I turned to look but nothing showed. When I turned back, I saw the sergeant leaking blood from his chest. "Get out!" he ordered before collapsing onto one knee.

The miners fled immediately without any hesitation, the only issue was that their retreat was in all directions. I grabbed the sergeant's shoulder, "Come on, get on your horse!" I shouted at him.

He was poised with extreme strain. His one knee dug into the earth below as the other supported his weight. The sergeant had the rifle pressed against his shoulder, the bad one, with his eyes glaring down the sights. "Get out," he said calmly.

Roars of pain and fear erupted from the forest followed by the trademark screams and cries of the contaminated. Voices shouting as they were being torn apart. Gunshots fired sporadically as the men and women of the mine tried to defend themselves. One ran into view. It was a broad shouldered man with blood streaming down his arm - cut wide open with flaps of skin whipping around as he ran. "More!" he shouted as he saw us. "Humans helping the contaminated! Those crazy ass-" POP-POP the sergeant's gun went off as the contaminated pursuer appeared behind the miner, dropping the contaminated immediately. The man nodded at the sergeant in thanks. He turned to flee when a hole the size of a water bottle exploded from his chest. The miner flopped to the ground without even a twitch of movement.

"Those crazy shits are here," I said quietly to the sergeant. He was pale, way too pale to sustain life for much longer. His body was being deprived of blood. I pulled a knife hidden in my boot and slashed a piece of my flannel shirt off. Before he could object, I shoved the piece into his wound in an effort to stop the bleeding.

The sergeant grunted in pain but acknowledged me with a quick nod. "My chances of getting out of this are a lot better with you around. Get on your horse," I demanded.

The sergeant looked as if he was about to shoot me, his face crinkling from lack of superior respect. Before he got the chance to shoot me, I wrapped my left arm under his armpit and hoisted him onto his feet. He was weak. My body could barely support all of his own.

Whether it was just stupid or obedient, the sergent's horse hadn't fled the scene. With a power unbeknownst to myself, I managed to get the sergeant onto his steed. He was half slumped over in the saddle, rifle still amazingly at the ready.

Before I could hop on, two more contaminated were darting towards me. I knew I'd pay for it if I managed to live, but I stabbed the sergeant's horse in the rear with my knife. The horse whinnied in pain and darted off towards the exit of the woods. I believe the sergeant yelled something about a 'little shit-snack.'

I quickly raised my rifle as the contaminated approached. My body was strategically between two trees and a presentation of prickly bushes preceded them, giving me a wonderful spot to wedge my enemies into. The contaminated mindlessly ran with all of their might towards me, raging and screaming their heads off as a fresh meal was ready and seasoned right in front of them.

They dropped in three shots, the first of which penetrated the first and impaled into the second's shoulder. The second shot was just sloppy on my part. I took two steps forward before something hard hit me on the back of the head, splitting my vision with an electrical line of light flaring up across my eyes. My body fell to the ground before I had time to react.

"No moving," a voice hissed from behind me. My rifle was within reach, but as I tried to creep my hand up to it, a pair of boots kicked it away, followed quickly by stomping down on my hand with an excruciating crunch.

A pair of legs with tightly strapped boots appeared in front of me. I ignored the order of fnot moving and sat up. I was already disarmed, my rifle being scattered a few paces away and my handgun in the grasp of one of my assailants.

"How should we do this?" one man asked the other. It was only two of them, though I figured there would be more hidden in the woods. "Call the others," he commanded.

The man with the tightly strapped boots brought his fingers up to his lips and whistled loudly. Two figures emerged from the forest. Each had camo jackets and pants as well as military grade boots. It was the two guards sent out to scout. "Took you long enough!" one of the guards said.

"What's going on?" I asked out of place. I was fortunate they laughed at my question instead of shoving a boot into my teeth as a reply.

One of the scouts spoke up, "The lords have blessed us on this day with a great feast!" The man had deep eyeblack swathed around much of his face. It made him seem like a skeleton, with deep receding eyes. "Where are the rest? It is time for someone's first blessing!"

"May I have a turn, Marvin," the other military scout asked. He had less eyeblack skewing his face but made up for it with green and grey muddy designs on his cheeks. "I have been a good soldier for you, bringing you many blessings. May i receive my first blessing?"

Marvin stood, "I have been handing out too many blessings of late. A few weeks ago, one of our loyal subjects was given a blessing. Some brat with a mouth got the best of her unfortunately. The freak named his weapons too. Can't remember the douchebag's name though."

I smirked quietly before becoming sullen. It sounded like an old friend.

Before I had time to reminisce much longer, a snarling, screaming contaminated showed up being led by another of the freaks. I had no doubt that these were members of the CRU, Contaminated 'R' Us as dubbed by -, but I had never heard any reports of them being so close to actual contaminated. Reports always said that they would have to hide from the mutants as well as hungry contaminated would not hesitate to kill anyone not contaminated. This was different. This was a man directly leading a contaminated monster through the woods and to my position. Were the other contaminated who attacked earlier guided by the same people as well?

The soldier held out his arm to the contaminated's mouth and rolled back his sleeve. The contaminated bared its teeth, stretching its lips back as far as they could go before chomping down on the soldier's arm. It ripped a piece of peeling flesh which looked like a piece of human colored plastic melting. The soldier barely cried out in pain, just a subtle wince as the teeth removed the arm contents up to the bone. The contaminated tore its blood stained mouth away from the chunk of man, swallowing hard without even a hint at chewing.

"I've - gah - been...blessed," the soldier said as his arm was drenched in blood from the wound. Marvin handed the soldier a white rag which he promptly placed over his bite mark. The white rag quickly turned red. It seemed as if it barely slowed the bleeding - if at all.

I decided to speak seeing as my future was looking less and less - appetizing. "What's the blessing for?" I inquired, not talking to anyone in particular. "What does a blessing do for a man?"

"Man or woman," the creep called Marvin spoke up. There was an air of superiority about him. It wasn't enough to make him the CRU leader but certainly gave him some authority. "Anyone may be blessed by the lords above or below. The blessing is the evolution serum, what our transformed brethren have inside of themselves, to bless upon us with. It is undoubtedly a way that we petty humans can become more than just ourselves, a way to transform and *evolve* into a better species." He walked slowly towards me, his thick soled boots crunching dried leaves and twigs with each step. "The first blessing is the meal that our brothers receive when they first evolve. You shall be that good man's first blessing," Marvin said as he pointed to the soldier.

My heart shriveled up to the size of a raisin. The pressure in my chest meant that I probably was not getting out of this alive. My limbs were not bound, but with all of these CRU along with the contaminated around, there was no chance at escape. I did the only thing I could think of to survive, "How can I become blessed?"

Marvin threw back his head, weaving a gloved hand through his dark bowl cut hair. "You have lost that opportunity!" he said as he whipped his head back into place. His eyes were wide and staring at me. I could have sworn they were a shade of yellow, or diarrhea brown.

I did my best kitten impression with my own, "But sir, I never had a chance! I only wish to serve the lords above and below." I averted my gaze as if I was ashamed of myself. "I only ever wanted to serve, nothing more. I can be an asset to you, to your - our - cause. I have been inside the walls of Kansas City. I can be an inside man for the lords!"

Marvin shrugged, "We have people inside, as expressed here," he said pointing to the two soldiers. "We could always use more, but I don't think that's really necessary right now. There are enough followers on the inside I think. If I'm not mistaken, which I never am, then I'd say-"

Something flickered out of the corner of my eye, then everything turned to white with a loud ringing. I was blinded by the noise, my hands wanting to rip my ears off of my head. I thought someone was shouting - something about their back. I thought I heard guns firing, but I didn't know for sure. Everything was too white.

*   *   *   *

*   *

"Quiet!" I whispered harshly. Mattheiu crinkled dried leaves with each passing step. I was just thankful that the horses were not making a noise. Mattheiu had a sack of carrots with him which he was basically shoving down the horses' throats in order to keep them quiet.

I felt his hand creep on my shoulder, "Can you see any of them, Chelsea?"

Before we left him, the sergeant gave me a really nice, large rifle with a sick-ass zoom on it. It had infared and all of the goods along with bullets the size of your mother's sex toys. This thing was ready to rip through a tree and whoever took cover behind it.

I flicked off the infrared as it was annoying to look at. Nobody out in the woods was hiding. They figured we all fled in outrageous fear! My sights were lined up to some guy talking. He didn't look armed, just like a douchebag. "Circle around the," I whispered to Matthieu. "Here," I handed him a flashbang. He gave a look as if he wanted more, "We need to conserve what we have. We can't just go banging around everywhere."

He shrugged, "Yeah but situations like these are why we conserve the weapons, so that we can use them when we have to." I gave him another. He nodded in approval. Matthieu went off without another word. The port bellied man lumbered off into the forest quieter than I'd imagined possible for him. I hoped that his chrome head wouldn't reflect the sun into our enemies' eyes.

After what seemed like two years, Matthieu's forever balding head signaled his position to me. None of the others seemed to notice. I looked to my side to see the horses' heads stuck inside the carrot bag. I ripped the bag from under them and threw it deep into the woods in the direction of our attacker. The poorly trained steeds galloped off after it without hesitation. *See the signal,* I said to myself as I raised the sights to my eye.

The contaminated was the first target I'd take down. I wasn't sure how it would react to a flashbang and I was not going to take any chances. Two glittering barrels of freedom soared through the air and into the middle of the encampment. Sputtering flakes of white magnesium erupted from the canisters along with a defaning BANG! My bullet followed in conjunction with the eruption of the grenades. The contaminated's head was ripped open, flying in all directions as everyone else in the vicinity raked at their eyes in pain.

One of the soldiers with his arm wrapped in a bloodied cloth stepped into view. He was rubbing his eyes with one hand and waving around a handgun with the other. The red crosshairs found him quickly. Before I could pull the trigger, the other soldier stepped into view. "Yes, plese," I pulled the trigger hard. The scene unfolded in beautiful sixty-thousand frames per second slow motion. The bullet penetrated the first soldier, gouging a hole in his chest the size of a coffee mug (like those 20 oz ones) and sputtered through the other soldier, giving him a whole new exciting orifice.

The remaining CRU were hidden behind the vegetation. These woods were old, tall oaks with trunks as wide as the tire of a yellow construction plow with prickly bushes covering the in-between.

Matteiu stumbled into view. One hand was caressing his back as the other held a six-shot revolver at the ready. He caught up to Zach, looping one arm through the blinded boy's own. Zach flailed for a second before realizing who was helping him up. Matteiu hoisted Zach up but fell to one knee as his back flared up. Zach was rubbing his eyes, trying to wipe the white noise away from them.

There was a sudden roar as a contaminated rushed through a gap in the trees, but this roar was close. I twisted around to see a jacked up contaminated rushing me. Its body was engorged and the flesh was a deep sunburnt red. The contaminated had no shirt on, as its body was too big to fit into one. It just had a pair of sweatpants tied in a bow at the waist. The monster had no hair on its head, but small dark streaks of fur were lining its arms. This was an in between contaminated, the middle ground between basic contaminated and colossal contaminated.

There was no time to turn and aim the rifle. I twisted in place, holding the weapon like a spear against my chest to brace for the impact. The contaminated lowered its massive shoulder and crashed into me hard. The wind was instantly knocked out of me as my body flew backwards. I somehow managed to stay on my feet, gasping for any form of oxygen to reach my lungs.

The contaminated was on me again, a relentless crazing rush. It was like a bull seeing red, only this contaminated probably would have taken the bull by the horns and crushed it.

I rolled out of the way of the next charge, the contaminated crashing into a tree and rattling it of its needles from the impact. My rifle lay at the contaminated's feet, giving me no chance at that. I drew a knife from the inside of my boot and held it at the ready. The contaminated didn't even take notice. It charged with the full ferocity it had the first time. I rolled again to the side and whipped the blade around. The steel kissed flesh, cutting the contaminated deep. It collapsed and rolled but was back on its feet in an instant.

I needed that rifle to beat this thing.

I booked it towards the weapon lying at the base of a large oak. There was no time - I made my mistake. The contamianted was too fast for me. This wasn't well planned, this poor strategy of mine. I needed the rifle to win, but going right for it was only getting me killed.

My life was ending, here and now. At least it wasn't so bad. I took down a bunch of the fuckers in the process.

Right as the contaminated was about to crush me with another charge, a large portion of its head erupted in split bone and jiggly gore. Two more shots filled its chest before the monster collapsed.

"Are you alright?" Matteiu asked. His gun still had smoke pouring out of the exit hole. Zach was leaning against him, his eyesight slowly returning to normal. "Get off, please," Matteiu said through gritted teeth as his back undoubtedly flared.

Zach fell to me, hugging me tight. "Don't scare me like that," he said. "You know how much I hate bright lights."

*   *   *   *
*   *

"How're you doing, Sir?" I asked the sergeant in his hospital room a few weeks after the mining incident. He apparently didn't have many visitors which was totally unsurprising to me as he was such a personable - person.

He looked at me through weary eyes, "Doing good, Zach. You did well out there."

"Thanks, sir. Are your wounds healing well enough? I know there was a lot of delay on your recovery as setbacks really hindered you."

He scoffed, "Well, I pushed myself a bit hard I guess. Who knew wounds would just open up like that after lifting a few weights. Shit just gushes out once those stitches snap." He smiled and extended his hand, "Call me Adrian." I took it and returned the firm handshake. "Adrian when we're in private, but if you call me anything but sergeant in front of people, I'll be sure you will take my place here in the hospital."

I snorted in laughter, hoping he was joking. "Why did you call me here, Adrian?"

"I'm going to be pushing it a bit soon, and I'll need competent help," he said. "Once I'm out of this shithole, I'm moving out. The chancellor is the only person with any authority on the subject, and one of the few who helped develop the plan."

"The governor assigned this operation to you?" I was stunned. The chancellor ran a tight ship, being the leader of Kansas City and humanity's salvation. He was rarely seen in public, from what I heard. My eyes had never seen him. The man was so concerned with being attacked, he rarely left his highly guarded office. "How did you manage to meet the governor?"

Adrian waived me off, "That doesn't matter. What matters is accomplishing this mission for the chancellor. We're exploring the wild. It is apparent that the terroristic threat of these crazed people is greater than we imagined. Humanity has underestimated, well, humanity. We need to learn more about these people, the extremists without a name."

"The Contaminated 'R' Us, or CRU for short," I chimed in. "An old friend dubbed them."

Adrian smiled wide, revealing abnormally white teeth, "I like it. I'll make a notion next time we're at a naming ceremony for these shits." He rubbed his chest beneath the white gown where the wound was. "Needless to say, our civilization needs more intelligence on the CRU. They're part of the reason humanity is in the shit it's in. Why don't we go about learning how to remove the shit?"

"Who do you have for the team?" I asked interested. Before we finally settled down here, I enjoyed being on my own. There was some thrill living in constant fear which really made me want to shit my pants while running from contaminated again.

Adrian's eyes dimmed, "Unfortunately, I can't trust anyone, well almost no one. I had two betrayals by my own men, guys I deemed fit to watch my back. And they just left me, probably shot me, knowing all along what they were planning. I had no idea, that's what pisses me off more than anything. It pisses me off knowing full well that I could have chosen two others for guard duty, but I allowed their request to go through. Volunteers are always better than those forced to go. Might need to change that now." His dark brown eyes were distantly staring through the window at nothing.

I fake did my best impression of a fake cough, snapping the sergeant into place. "Anyway, I only have three true candidates, three useful ones anyway. You, Mateiu, and Chelsea. I already approached Chelsea. She was here right before you. I won't tell you her decision as she asked me not to until you gave a response. I asked Matteiu. He's on the rocks, his back still bothering him. The man has a quality shot and knows some survival techniques as well which is quite convenient. So that leaves you."

"I'm in," I replied without a second thought.

"Can I ask why?" Adrian - asked.

My fists were clenched, tightening harder than before. If I didn't bite my nails, they would have pierced the skin on my palm. I noticed that my body was shaking from anger and pent up rage, "They killed my friend, a goddamn good friend who did everything in his power to be sure Chelsea and I made it this far. I'm going to fuck those CRU up. I already know Chelsea's response, her motivation to go with you. We are going to avenge Daryll Willows."

CHAPTER 5 - DENVER

I was close now. The Rockies were in sight, their sky piercing peaks drenched in icy powered snow. They meshed with the sky being the largest thing in sight. These things were undoubtedly the tits of America.

I thought the area reeked of pollution, but there's no way that was possible seeing how nothing was really running anymore. I'd passed abandoned power plants in my travels. The eerie smoke stacks merely holding their places until someone came along to reclaim their former peaking glory.

The only unfortunate part about this trek to Colorado was that the roads were no longer in the process of being plowed. I was essentially blind, making my frantic search across the frozen wilderness one of many dangers. I'd go days without seeing any signs of civilization, and nowadays they are just that: signs. No scantily clad women greet you at their doors with a hot tray of muffins and steaming cup of coffee. The places were empty, a depressing empty where the visions of life are evident, the only missing piece is life in the present.

The only liveliness in my life was Milly and Chetty. Neither were exceptional at conversation.

The middle of nowhere was really starting to get to me. Bland white knee-deep flat wilderness was nothing short of beautiful, but this kind of beauty is meant for a passerby's glance, not the eternal walk of damnation. My eyes only knew how to stare ahead, straight ahead at the same damn mountain off in the distance which never seemed to grow in size. Either this was the world's first shrinking mountain, or progress was taking forever.

Whipping winds lashing against my core chilled body did

not help matters in the slightest. My body was frozen to the core. My spectacular boots were the only reason my feet hadn't fallen off. It still amazed me how they could keep my feet dry in such harsh environments.

I pulled out a paper map, arguably the last paper map in the United States. Really, though, I must have searched every building in Milwaukee on my way out for this damn thing. My foot finally busted down a locked door to a nice little cottage which must have belonged to the cutest old couple to ever exist. There were a bunch of those 'Jesus Loves You' pillows and little hand knit sayings of prayer messages. With a lacking knowledge of the internet, I had no doubt that this elderly couple had used the map for its actual purpose.

It was a little saddening, breaking into the abandoned house of the old couple. I didn't know them, but there was an air about the house which really made me feel at home. There were no pictures hanging, and I did not spend the time searching for details of the owners, but being there in that house was the first time I really felt like I belonged somewhere. I nearly considered staying in the confines of the home and living out the rest of my days there. But I would have gone mad, being alone for so long. I named my god damn weapons just so that I could have some semblance of companionship. I'd hate to see what I would do if I lost one.

The map flapped harshly in the wind. I quickly crumpled it up and made a small barrier out of snow using a small spade I found in a survival store. I rounded the mound at the top and patted it into place before squatting down to shield myself from the wind as well. The edges of the map flapped a bit as I opened it again, but it fortunately held its shape.

I still had a very long way to go, and that was only if I was totally on course. By my estimates, I was covering somewhere between twenty and thirty miles per day. If the snow didn't come up to my knees constantly, I would be far closer to Denver than I was. There were at least one hundred miles left on my journey, by my guess it could be more than double that number. I was almost positive that at the worst, I was still in Nebraska. Mountains were on all sides of my position, the Rockies taking up the majority, but the hills of South Dakota were visible to my right. That was the epitome of an encouraging sight. Fortunately for me, a small town should be coming into view within a few hours. I needed a small town to come into view. I had very little remaining food left. My stores of dried beef were rapidly running thin in an effort to keep fueling my body's constantly decreasing temperature.

Welcome to Stratton! The large green aluminum road sign said. That was all, no motto, no catchphrase or anything. Just a nice entrance to Stratton Nebraska. This confirmed to me that I was still about two hundred miles out from Denver, more if I somehow managed to follow the roadway.

This place was the definition of a small town. There were main roads, the highway running right through the southern side and one perpendicular to that. I saw a Catholic church on my way in and another church smack in the middle of town. The town was small enough, and the land flat enough, to where I could see to the end of the glorified village before I stepped foot in it.

I ventured into a small coffee shop. The hospitality of the store greeted me with cobwebs and a lack of fresh coffee. The chairs were resting on the table tops, all except for one. One sole loosley cushioned chair was sitting on all fours against the counter. It looked like whoever closed up shop last had one final cappuccino.

My finger fiddled with the light switch. Unfortunately there was no power here, and it was still freezing cold. I found a grill in the back area. Propane was attached and the canister was not empty. I was counting my blessings. The tank squealed as the lever turned. I flicked the gas setting too high and opened up my lighter. The grill was quickly alight, warmth finally spreading throughout my body.

I went outside and stuffed a pot full of snow before returning it to the grill. The icy whiteness began to instantly melt. Once it was gurgling water, I threw in some potentially stale coffee beans. I could not wait for it to fully boil. A white rose mug was sitting on the countertop. Without even considering if it was clean or not, I dunked it into the steaming water, retrieving some of the dark liquid for my body to take.

It had been a long time since I had consumed anything this hot, and thusly burned my throat as the coffee went down. It was good though, really good. The fresh taste of bitter black coffee grinds filled my taste buds with spewing caffeine. I always did brew the best coffee.

Darkness was beginning to settle in. The orange sun was still up, but its glow was severely weakening. Deep shades of fruit orange pressed through the tops of the mountains as the sun began to lose its power. I had maybe an hour of sunlight left at best.

I needed to find a way to move, a way to move with speed. I couldn't be sure if there was any sign of civilization coming up, anything which I could survive off of. This small coffee place had enough food for me for a while, and the snow was very good at melting when warmed. My biggest fear was falling from exhaustion, or falling asleep without adequate heat. The last thing that I wanted was to freeze to death.

I remembered passing a farm on my way in. There had to be something usable there.

The door to the coffee shop opened with the ringing of bells. I looked up to see a yellow sign: Stratton Grill. "Huh? Sorry about that," I said to the grill. "For a grill, you sure do make a decent cup of coffee."

I pressed down the main roadway towards the farm. It was not too far, seeing as the town couldn't have been larger than a square mile. But before I reached the edge of Stratton, a gurgling rumble came from my side. I turned to see an open door and a contaminated walking out of it. This thing was dead, well more than normal anyway. The pale flesh was skin-tight, wrapped against the bone. I had never met an anorexic contaminated, but this is what one would look like if I had. There was a lone wisp of hair swirling with the chilling breeze at the top of its head. The contaminated wore jeans which were more like ankle cuffs as they sagged to the knees. The sleeveless shirt it had was more like torn rags hanging on to dear life like a desperate ex-girlfriend (or boyfriend, I guess). It limped towards me with a renewed lack of energy.

I had all the time in the world to draw Chetty from her sheath. The glistening hardened steel glowed red in the sun's embrace. There was little more to do than walk up to the contaminated and cut it down, but the caffeine coursing through my body wouldn't have any of that quiet nonsense. I charged the contaminated with newfound energy, doing a showy roll past it. The machete flew through the air like a rose petal, slicing off a section of the contaminated's remaining leg muscle. I did a half twirl. The blade crunched against the spinal column and tore through the remaining muscle fortified by cartilage. The contaminated fell without another whimper. Dark oozing purple-red blood soaked the snow, turning it into an appetizing looking snowcone.

"What are you doing here?" I asked the deceased contaminated. Knowing full well that I was not getting a reply, I continued. "You're the first contaminated I've seen in three states. No others are in the town, though to be fair I haven't gone into the churches yet, scoff!" (I actually said scoff out loud?!?!).

I turned in place. The town was as quiet as ever. There had not been any noise since I came to Stratton. The only thing I could think of was that the contaminated showed up when I was making that outstanding cup of coffee, but as loud as boiling water is, I should have heard it grumbling in.

I shook off the idea. The contaminated was probably just one remaining from when this shit all went down. It probably fed off of the corpses of the town before getting lost here (in the not even a square mile town. What an idiot).

Still in a good mood from having coffee for the first time in many moons, I began to briskly stroll down the street, whistling 'Hooked on a Feeling.'

The farm was in plain view, as everything around here was

pretty much just one big plain. Much of the farm was covered with snow, but the house was still standing as was the barn and granary. I wanted to stop in the house to see what supplies it held, but the barn was more important right now. I needed a way to travel faster, other luxuries would come next.

I reached the barn entrance. White chipped paint crossed between the peeling maroon barn colors. The hinges were once painted black, but were now a rusted brown with glossy black highlights. The barn itself was two stories tall, no doubt a second level for storage held numerous bales of hay.

The latch wretched as I pushed it to unlock the door, grinding against the wood frame. I pulled hard on the barn doors, but they merely gave a half-hearted response. Even though the snow was powder, it still proved enough resistance when working in conjunction with the less than ideal hinges. Lacking a shovel, I was forced to kick the snow aside. After an epic kung-fu battle with the wintery earth, I was finally able to swing the door open just wide enough to squeeze inside.

The barn was mostly empty. The interior held a few tools such as a hoe, metal rakes, a pick axe, and other assorted farm goods. Hay was everywhere, even still in tightly wrapped bushels piled three or four high. I climbed to the second floor via a wooden ladder. The yellow grass called hay was thrown up here and strewn about. There was no rhyme or reason to the placement, just scattered vegetation.

It was dark in here. The sun was nearly below the horizon and the barn doors didn't allow much light to get in. The barn provided a strange warmth, a comforting feeling of ease. I threw up my hood and lay down on the piles of hay. Something hard stabbed into my back. When I reached back, I pulled out a pump-action shotgun. *Nice.* I checked the chamber. It was loaded already. I'd try it out sometime soon. For now, the warmth and comfort was overwhelming. I fell into a deep sleep.

At least I thought it was a deep sleep. I was awoken by the sound of rolling thunder, but this was winter, so it obviously wasn't thunder. A 'YIP' and a 'YAP' echoed across the plains of

Stratton. Men on horses were approaching (or women, jeez). I quickly got to my feet only to stumble and trip over the shotgun I found, the barrel smashing into my shins. Searing heated pain shot through my lower legs as I was no doubt in for some bruising.

I quickly recovered and readied the shotgun to my shoulder. The barrel of the weapon was aimed directly at the barn door. I hope this thing worked and didn't just explode in my hands.

But the yipping and yapping merely passed down the street in the distance. Being that it was still night, they probably wouldn't notice the barn door open just a nudge. Either that or the passerbys simply didn't care, which meant that they brought a great arrogance about them. I hated arrogant people.

I pulled the chamber of the shotgun back quickly to check the round before realizing that it was pitch dark inside the barn at this late hour. After sliding the chamber back into place, I crept along the barn wall. Everything inside of me was saying to stay in the barn and wait it out, but everything else was telling me to investigate.

I reached the ladder and quickly climbed down, sliding the last few rungs. My arm bumped into something leather. I felt around and had no idea what it could be, so I grabbed hold of the cold object and thrust it out into the moon's glow. *Saddlebags!* were of no use to me unless I had something to saddle. The men lumbered in on something which wasn't powered by an engine though, and considering basic bicycles didn't make such a noise, I'd take the Vegas odds on them riding in on horseback.

The hay beneath me was nearly frozen to the touch and littered with snow. I had to go deeper into the barn in order to find looser hay without having to climb back to the second level. I stuffed the saddlebags to the brim with hay and threw it over my shoulder. The bag was heavy, very heavy now filled with horse food. I had to slog through the snow with the immense pressure on my back combined with the backpack filled with supplies, Milly and Chetty who have never heard of a diet, and now my new shotgun friend. I need to stop naming these things.

So began my long not-so-long trek to where the horses remained. I followed the tracks through the snow, seeing as that was really not difficult. The tracks followed a straight path for a short while before cutting down a street. I followed until I reached a church. It was a small church. Its peak rose high above the stained glass depictions of Mother Mary and Jesus Christ. A small brass bell hung inside the peak but did not sound.

Seven horses were tied to a post in the dirt parking lot, or presumably dirt parking lot - there was too much snow to really tell. Of the seven, only three looked healthy. These must have been a different breed of horse, ones which were built for distance travel while the others were more for speed.

I crept over to a horse with brown fur and white patches all over its body. The cliche name would simply be patches for my new friend, but I figured that pirates wore patches and this was a female horse. "Mary," I called my new companion as I threw the saddlebags on top of the saddle.

There was no reason to stay past that. I had the horse saddled with food. I had gone unnoticed by the people which I was stealing the horse from. I found a shotgun (in questionable repair) and had coffee earlier today. This was a good - no - great day. I just had to add some stress to it.

Instead of doing the sane thing and leaving with the horse, I strapped the shotgun to the horse pack (stupid) and crept over to the lower church windows (stupid). Dim light shone through the thick glass. The strangers had lit a few candles and two large torches placed near the altar. Five rows of pews were on each side of the church leading up to the illuminated section. White walls depicting the epics of Jesus' life surrounded the interior of the church topped off with a thatched roof. This thing was done if it ever caught fire.

"Thank you all for joining me here at the place of original christening," a voice said coming from the edge of the altar. The deep voice was holding a torch exploding with light. A crimson hood covered his head as well as the others' in the room. There were eight total, eight total humans that is. Three of them were shorter and presumably women based on their physique. Two of the burlier ones were holding back another person, their arms spread wide as they flailed in attempts to achieve freedom.

"This is the ultimate ceremony, the closest any of us have come to evolving into a deity. Six of us here have received the Lords' Favors, and we will be welcoming one more." One man in a pitch black cloak lowered his hood. The man standing atop the altar held out a maroon hood between both of his hands. "You will join is as a higher power, a deity among men and our brothers. Please, fellow lord, remove your cloak and embrace the power of the gods!"

The person who pulled off their cloak was actually not a man as I initially thought. The woman was tall, her hair dark and wavy reaching down to her shoulders. She wore a tight black tank top which emphasized her curves. Her lower half was covered by a loose fitting, yup, black dress which stopped just high enough to reveal her military grade boots.

She turned around to face the man wriggling in the grip of the others. It was then that the so-called man snarled and hissed. It was a contaminated that was being held back in the grip of two of the CRU members. One of the lead CRU slapped the contaminated hard on the spine. The monster instantly became docile. The burly men released the contaminated from their grasp, the monster simply standing, weaving back and forth as if it was a drunk trying to walk on a boat traversing rough surf.

The woman was in full view now. The majority of her pale face was hidden behind the shadow created by her hair. Only her pointed nose and pomegranate lips were visible through the darkness. So was her cleavage showing through the peak of the too tight tank top (fuck yeah alliteration). She was pretty, really really pretty. I had not been in contact with many women lately, and being in the prime of my fertility, this nearly set me off.

Then I remembered the necklace I wore around my - neck. Chelsea still had a place with me, no matter how hard I tried to let her go. I would probably never see her again, never feel her touch or annoyingly weave my hands through her silky soft hair. That was something I would have to come to terms with eventually, but I don't think I was ready yet. Not while this chain was around my neck. It would always belong to the one I loved.

The thought of Chelsea snapped me out of my trance. I peeked through again. This could be useful information, but a nagging thought inside of me kept telling me to leave.

I looked just in time to see the woman take a chunk out of the contaminated's neck. The contamination didn't even move. The woman spit the chunk of flesh from her mouth then began to rip apart the contaminated's flesh down through its chest. Her arms disappeared for a minute before reemerging, covered in blood up to the elbows. In her hands was the beating heart of the contaminated. Each beat of the pink-purple vomit of colors expelled blood. The woman lifted it to her lips and drank from the artery with each pulsation.

The situation made my stomach feel as if someone dropped a boulder inside of it. I tore my eyes from the window and began to sickly walk back to the horses. *Not here, please don't puke here. They'll hear (fuck yeah rhyming).* I managed to make it around the corner of the church before the dam broke. I vomited hardcore, projectile nearly two meters which, in hindsight, was awesome.

Somehow, I managed to recover after a few spurts of bile. The damage had been done though. The snow was a yellow-green lollipop flavor, and someone heard what happened.

I had no choice.

I leapt onto the horse in one leap, nearly heaving again, and pulled the machete from my back. Chetty came down on the leather straps holding the other horses to the posts right as a few enraged screams came from inside. The horses did not move an inch. "Move!" I shouted at them. The last thing that I wanted to do was kill an innocent animal just to secure my escape, but I would do what I had to in order to survive. I pulled out the shotgun resting in the saddlebags. Chetty sheathed insdie the leather casing in one swift movement as I steadied the shotgun into my bad, once bitten by a stupid-ass CRU freak, shoulder. "Move!" I tried again, but there was no time to delay.

I fired a blast from the gun sounding as if I was a pissed off Zeus. The buckshot round collided with the church door leaving a gap six inches wide. The horses finally scattered in whinnying fear, but mine was none too accustomed to the sound of gunfire. Mary kicked up in fear, nearly throwing me from the saddle. I managed to grab on to the hilt of the saddle before it was too late. I gained some courage and transferred my hand to the reins and pulled hard. The horse swiveled towards the road just as someone finally managed to pry the door open. I kicked Mary's haunches and the horse took off. I turned and loosed another round of shotgun shell into the church, missing my target horribly but giving my assailants such a fright that the night was filled with prayers of curses.

Mary rode hard into the night, our only guidance being the quiet moon above.

*   *   *   *

*   *

I can't recall how long we rode. Mary was trotting at a pace which would easily have doubled my own. The mare's hooves rocketed through the snow, kicking it away as if it was nothing but styrofoam. At this rate, I was sure to reach Denver in a day or two. It all depended on Mary now. The feed I had probably wasn't enough for an extended journey across this type of wilderness especially with the snow blocking or killing her main food source.

The moonlight was now gone, the dawning sun approached with the coming day. I must have fallen asleep at one point during the journey. I had no memory of making such progress. My body was freezing cold. Riding a horse at a greater height exposed me to the cutting wind just as much as walking, but the currents were no doubt stronger being just a bit higher off the ground.

It was time we took a break. Mary was no doubt exhausted and the cold must have been getting to her a bit as well. I grabbed the reins and pulled the mare to a slowing stop. I leapt off, nearly losing my balance as I landed on the powdered snow. My feet dug into the white dust reaching nearly up to my ankles. There really was no way for me to anchor my horse. While holding the reins, I dug a makeshift trough and filled it with hay. The mare quickly dipped her head down into the cold yellow-brown hay and began chomping away. "Mary, you are chewing like a cow." Mary didn't take notice.

While she was distracted, I began digging again. It was another hole in the snow reaching all of the way down to the frozen earth. I had no wood, and there was no way for me to have a sustainable fire in these conditions. I readied all of my supplies before starting anything. A small pile of hay was to my side. Next to it was a can of broth which I opened by stabbing it with my knife. I transferred the remaining hay from the saddlebags into my pack, deciding to burn the extra weight away. I cut the saddle bag into strips, giving me another way to tie and repair equipment.

The hay was piled high into the ditch. I pulled out one of my lighters and sparked it. The yellow flame quickly lit, and I plunged it into the hay den. As soon as the majority was alight, I threw the can of broth directly into the flame. Mary was nearly done with her less than sufficient meal. I took her reins and threaded them between my backpack which I was wearing. There was enough slack to allow her to remain comfortably distant as I tended to my needs.

Realizing my folly too late, the can of broth began to bubble and spit from where I opened it. I had no grabber or hot mitts with me, as they generally are not very good survival items. I drew Chetty and placed the flat of her blade perpendicular with the red hot aluminum can. I maneuvered the blade under the can and flicked it out of the fire. It landed in the snow a few feet away with a loud hiss. The can melted a decent layer of snow before it had no more heat to combat the snow with. I safely grabbed the can and swabbed the top with snow just so it wouldn't mutilate my lips. I drank the liquid quickly. It wasn't hot-hot, but it wasn't cold either. The chicken broth was a warm welcome in such a crap environment.

I drained the remnants of the can and sat by the dying fire. The coals left behind by the hay were still red but were quickly losing their power. Mary's wet nose nudged me on my cheek, leaving a cold mark of moisture. I scratched my hand along her snout and down her neck. "You are definitely one of my better finds, Mary." I said as the strap of Chetty's sheath snapped and fell into the snow. "I didn't mean any offence!" I clamored. Giggling to myself, I used pieces of the saddlebags which I stripped apart to fix the machete holder.

Once fixed, I looked at Mary with a bit of sadness. "Sorry girl, we have to keep moving." She acknowledged with a light whinny. The bits of hay were long depleted of their energy. There really was no longer any reason to stay here in the open winter. "Come on, I'll even walk a bit."

We walked maybe five miles before I began to tire. Even with the can of broth, my energy levels were nowhere near where they should have been. I reluctantly leapt back on Mary's back and consumed more of my dried meat reserves than I should have. It was the only thing that I could do to keep myself warm in this open expanse.

The sunlight was finally showing through. The only problem now was the blindingly white snow reflecting the sun's light into my eyes. I averted them, looking backwards into the distance which we came from. My face immediately changed from squinting to fearful. I kicked Mary hard on her haunches, the horse immediately taking off at a greater pace. "I'm sorry, girl, but we're being followed. Give it a bit more for our sake."

I gave a light kick every time Mary started to lose speed, urging her on faster. Her overall trotting speed almost doubled as she bounced and bounded through the snow. Multiple individuals dressed in maroon cloaks were on our heels. They couldn't have been more than a mile or two away. I was considering my options, because if they caught up to me, there was no way I'd lose them a second time.

I wanted to make a slow fuse bomb, something that may not have been super damaging, but would at least scare the shit out of their horses. There was only one idea I could think up, and it was more of a prayer than anything.

I still had the aluminum can from the soup I had this morning. I packed the bottom with hay until it was tight enough to evenly support the weight of a shotgun shell. With the casing face up in the can, I lit a cigarette (don't smoke kids, really I only had these for this situation. Smoking kills, as you may find out), and placed the lit boge into a slot I created in the side of the can just above the hay-line. I jumped out of the saddle as if I was thrown from it. I couldn't have my followers see me carefully climb down and place something into the snow. That would not be a very well executed surprise.

The cigarette would burn slowly. The slow fuse would help me in more ways than one. I would hopefully be successful with my makeshift bomb, but it would also allow me to judge the distance of my pursuers. It also had a shot at freaking their horses out and delaying their process even more. At worst this didn't work out and the heat wouldn't be enough to trigger the small explosion. I was no explosion expert. Don't judge me. You know who you are - you chemical engineers sitting at home laughing at my petty attempt.

If my guesstimation was anywhere near correct, then there was about twenty minutes before the bomb would explode.

I continued trotting through the snow as Mary kicked it aside as if it was nothing more than a mound of cotton balls.

The sound reached me far after the explosion happened. It was nothing more than an echoing shotgun blast reverberating between the open plains and mountainous ranges in the distance. I looked back to be severely disappointed. I think the plan worked, at least as far as I could tell it did. My eyesight was not nearly as good as it had been before all of those violent video games. The sun deciding to shine extra bright as it reflected off of the tanning snow and into my delicate eyes did not help at all either. The only real piece of information I received from my I.E.D. was that my pursuers were more accurately two miles off instead of one based off of the sound travel of the explosion, which gave me a nice little cushion.

I kicked Mary's haunches with my heels, spurring her forward. Their disarray was my only chance at escape. Mary shunted forward as fast as her chilling legs would carry her. I didn't know if a horse's lower leg could freeze, but I imagine so whence considering physics. The gallop brought me farther and farther into the frozen wasteland, and closer to my destination.

*   *   *   *   *

Horse feet *clobped* down the main highway leading up to Denver. Bright green signs unfaded from the sun clearly marked the Mile High city. I felt bad for Mary. She'd faithfully walked all of the way from creepy-ass Stratton to the doorway of Denver, some two hundred plus miles. I had been walking alongside her for the past two or three. There was no doubt that it slowed us down, but my pursuers were far enough back to the point that I hadn't seen them for two whole days.

Maybe they gave up.

The highway was abandoned. There wasn't even the cliche burning car with its nose crushed against the highway barricade from every single apocalypse movie ever. It was just another empty roadway across the expanse of the former United States.

Denver finally came into decent view. It was a city alright. How the hell was I supposed to find someone in this expanse? Contaminated no doubt littered the streets, probably decrepit ones who could barely move, but still.

"Mary, what Denver landmarks are in the city?" I asked the horse. She literally gave a shit reply. "I know there's the football stadium, maybe the baseball stadium too, but where else would my contact be?" I was talking to a horse.

The city is huge, as far as empty cities go. Thinking about it now, there really were no more large civilizations. Our people were hurting, humanity as a whole. This life really sucks. If there's no cure to stopping the contamination, we're probably doomed.

A wretch and snarl came from behind me. I stopped Mary,

holding on tightly to the reigns. Mary stutter stepped but didn't seem shaken. Whatever I heard couldn't have been too close.

My eyes scanned the horizon. We were surrounded by plains on all sides. The suburbs were behind us, the main of the city finally beginning to envelop us in a forest of buildings and abandoned shops. Nothing came into immediate view. I hopped onto Mary's back, my feet fitting nicely into the foot straps.

Off in the distance - it must have been at least a mile away - was a small pack of darkness moving hastily along the highway. My entourage had followed me this far, all the way from Stratton. I waved to them, seeing as it was only polite. I'm apparently famous in these parts. $20 autographs please.

"Wait," I said to Mary. "Where did that snarl come from before then?" Sound traveled, but that was a stretch for my pursuers' noise to make it this far.

My feet lightly slapped the horse's sides, spurring her forward at a light trot, slightly faster than a walk. We cruised past shattered shop windows, glass littered inside as looters most likely smashed it in.

I heard the growl again. It was definitely a contaminated, hiding in the depths of the vegetation or broken sales points. I tapped Mary's haunches once more.

We came to an intersection. I looked down the perpendicular street. It was wider and extended a long way. I twisted Mary's reins to the left and led her down that street. If I had a contaminated in pursuit, it would be best not to be caught off guard.

A mannequin was sticking out of a half shattered window. It was wearing a Denver Broncos orange and blue jersey, sliced across the numbers where it contacted the glass. It made me want a sports jersey. I had so many in my closet at home, but bringing those on a survival trip may have been seen to many as a waste - though I don't think the 'many' really have a say anymore.

I slid off (out) of (ha!) Mary, landing lightly on my feet. She was easily tethered to an old bike rack. I stepped inside of the store, a light crunch of boot on glass sounding. I had Chetty in hand. No, this was not the best idea for me to do. Wandering into a dark store after hearing the menacing growl of a beast which wants nothing more than to devour my spinal column is not a good idea. This isn't a poor-choice-encompassing horror story, but let's add a little suspense every now and again.

The interior was dark. I passed by a clothing rack, knocking into it. The rack *creaked* at me in response, though had little other effect. I was searching for anything green, something that could spark a little bit of familiarity.

My eyes finally lay on the goal. Resting alone on the rack to the far wall lined with hats was a grass-green cap with the Jets logo on the front. These guys were my hated boys, the ones I could always count on to let me down, and I loved them for it. Sports passions were weird that way. Some people would irrationally kill to defend their team's name for a sport which has no actual literal impact on their lives whatsoever barring weekly seasonal entertainment; and I was engrossed in it.

I pulled the cap over my head. It was a bit tight around the warm winter hat already covering my head, but this way I knew it wouldn't take off (irony).

There was some kind of stupid smile on my face when I lept out of the threshold and back onto the street.

Click! The twang of a spring tightening. Steady breathing. "Move a muscle and I'll shoot that shit hat from your head."

CHAPTER 6 -
MANHATTAN OF
THE MIDWEST

"Four horses trotting in a row, swinging their tails to and fro, something something gotta know."

"Private Poet," the tall dark man said sitting atop his checkered steed. He held the reins with his left arm, moving his right very gingerly when needed.

"Yes, Sarge," I replied with a half salute.

Sarge sighed, "Adrian, call me Adrian. I'm not into the formalities as much as before. No real need to keep you guys 'in line' seeing as if you fall out of line you are most certainly dead." He adjusted his grip on the reins, forcing him to move his injured shoulder. If I wasn't staring directly at his face, the flicker of a grimace would have never been noticed crossing his lips.

"That being said, we don't need you to start a poetry club by bringing a couple of contaminated along with you. Got it, Zach?"

"Yeah - yeah, that's fine. But why's the poetry club gotta be mine? And what's the deal with turpentine?"

Adrian pulled a handgun from his holster, "I will shoot you, you pimple pioneer."

"Alliteration!" I said in a quiet shout. "Welcome on board, Sarge."

"Adrian," he corrected me.

Mattieu pulled up next to us. He was himself, bald on top with muddy brown hair lagooning the remainder of the scalp.

Disproportionately small murky green eyes poked through the front of his face to be met by round lense glasses. His portly belly was covered by a green and white checkered button down, muffin topping his jeans held up by a black leather belt. Mattieu's free hand itched his nose where it met with the moustache atop his upper lip.

"How's the back feeling?" Chelsea asked two horses down.

Mattieu shrugged, "Could be worse. Sitting on this horse forces me to have good posture so the back should be okay for now. I'm sure I'll pay for this plea of fortune somehow," he said in a kind, well spoken manner.

"Where are we headed, Sarge?" I asked. THere was a split decision to call him Adrian, but I knew him as Sarge and wanted it to remain that way.

He shook his head, "West, then North. We got a couple of cities westward, though I'm pretty sure the CRU would be somewhere remote, somewhere that the contaminated population would be down. They'll be wanting to spread the plague's influence where it isn't, and that is where we will gain information on them."

"What about their headquarters?" Chelsea asked.

Mattieu chimed in, "Headquarters wouldn't be smart, especially with four of us. This is just an intelligence reconnaissance mission. If we keep strict to our mission parameters, we'll be just fine. It's when you avert from your goal that the bad things start happening."

"Well said, Mattieu," Sarge commented. "If, as he said, the mission goes wrong and we don't look straight at the objective, shit's going down. I really would rather shit not go down when we're hundreds of miles away from Kansas City."

"So, moral of the story: less cities, more rural. Stick to the plan," I summed.

Sarge tucked his lips and shrugged, "Rural is certainly possible, but I'm thinking more village sized areas. Somewhere entirely off the map where the army would never have thought to look. Remember, when this whole thing first started, the military was really going after the CRU hard. Shit heads fought back hard too. The problem was how vulnerable the military was in the cities which is where all of the attacks happened. And checking on people - that was the worst part. An armywoman would ask someone to open their mouth for a swab only to get a bloody bite on the arm. Shit was really messed up. It was similar to how car bombs were going off at the checkpoints overseas. Sometimes there were car bombs filled with cut up humans, preserved in plastic bags just so that the moisture would hold out for the explosion. Survivors had no idea that the bloody shrapnel wasn't just their own. Breakouts happened. The contaminated kind. Hospitals went up fast. Security wasn't tight enough there. No way they could know. I just wish-"

"Sarge," I cut him off. "Were you in the middle of this?"

He gave me a deep look. Not one of anger, but actually sadness. "That's for another time." Sarge readjusted himself in the saddle. "We got a town coming up. We can do a quick sweep, though I don't want to linger long. The CRU had to have a camp somewhere nearby. They planted people, agents, in KC."

"What if they just made a quick camp in the woods?" Chelsea asked.

"That's why I want it to be a quick sweep."

"What town?" I asked.

"Manhattan."

My mind instantly went to New York, "Manhattan isn't on our way - not even close. Unless this journey is going to be much longer than I initially signed on for."

Sarge smirked, "You're not from around here. There's another Manhattan - Manhattan Kansas. It's actually a place, and not a small one. Actually it's kind of a bigger city."

"Why are we searching for it? I thought we were looking into smaller towns."

"A big town is a good place to hide, private poetry. As I said, they probably had a camp somewhere. Let's find it."

Manhattan was big, well not huge but still big. It was like the actual Manhattan minus the buildings hiding their tops in the overcast and the over congestion of literally everything. Cars weren't swamping the streets and it didn't smell like roasting piss. I could get used to this Manhattan.

We swept through the city quickly. Chelsea and Sarge went to their own party as I paired up with Mattieu. "Not complaining, but why are you going with Chelsea?" I asked Sarge.

He shrugged, "This way if something happens to you, she won't have to be a hero to save your ass. Mattieu, make sure his ass doesn't need saving."

"Pretty sure I saved your ass..." I mumbled as Mattieu and I paired up.

We stuck to two main roads shooting through the city. Serge and Chelsea went along STREET while Mattieu and I went down STREET. We rationalized, in such a desolate town, the CRU probably would make a base camp somewhere with ease of access. No reason to make a camp somewhere that wasn't easy to get to when the only occupants in the town are the CRU.

The town was wildly unoccupied as one might imagine. Cliche WASP houses lined the side streets, visible from the main. Strip malls and smaller one story buildings were in an array lining STREET. Shops had windows busted out as per the usual when it came to abandoned towns. I could see myself living here once upon a time ago.

Mattieu and I passed by the upteenth deli as we rode through. 'Marvin's Stop to Go' the unlit sign read.

"Check this out," Mattieu said as we passed by the only roadside shop without a plethora of smashed windows. I pressed my nose against the cold glass. "That's a campfire in there. Someone was recently here."

I pulled my nose away from the window, leaving a greasy mark. "How do you know that was recent?" I asked.

Mattieu shrugged, "I don't. But we are searching for people in this area and this is a camp which may have belonged to them. So why don't we investigate?"

"No need for sass."

"That was not sass, Zach," Mattieu said with a hint of a

smile.

Mattieu pushed the door open harshly. Golden bells attached to a chain clattered and rang with the motion. A 9 millimeter black handgun entered the store right before he did. I followed two paces behind, six shooter at the ready.

"Service," I said loosely. Mattieu glared at me. "It would be nice for any contaminated to come out before we're ambushed."

Mattieu took two steps forward. The store was lined with racks of clothing. Some department store, probably an expensive name brand that the kids are all supposed to gawk over to look cooler than the person next to them who happens to have a shirt without the name on it. "I always hated places like this," Mattieu said. "My daughter, she loved them. However-" but he stopped suddenly. "Look."

I stepped forward, staggered, but regained my balance before falling on top of a corpse. Two people lay curled up next to what was their campfire. Their heads rested on large stuffed packs. Each person had a heavy winter coat on along with matching fur hats.

Mattieu pulled the fuzzy brown hat off of the closest one, "A woman, and from the looks of things, so is the other body." He bent down and gently caressed the woman's cheek, "We need to see what is in these packs. Do you have an issue touching a dead body? They are cold at this point."

I shook my head. The woman laying silently had her eyes closed, pale flesh matching the color of the snow outside. She looked like Chelsea for a moment, pulling my heart from my chest. "I'll get the other one," I said quietly. I had to get used to corpses. That's how the world is now.

Her eyes were closed. *She looks so kind and warm*, I remember thinking. I gently reached down and cupped her face, the cold frozen jaw resonating its lack of warmth to my palm. My muscles gently moved, lifting the unknown maiden's head off of her pack and gently resting it on the floor.

"What do you think happened to them?" I asked.

Mattieu shrugged, "Probably carbon monoxide poisoning. It

fits the bill. No visible wounds, a fire clearly producing the gas, and two bodies. Unless it was a physical poison, but I don't have my lab stuff for that."

"You worked in a lab?"

Mattieu rolled his eyes a bit, "Biology professor, but this isn't the time for that story." He hastily unzipped the pack, pulling out contents left and right. Once it was fully empty, Mattieu took stock, "Two pants, two shirts, heavy wool socks, one pen, one notebook. What was in yours?"

"The exact same stuff," I replied. "That's not fishy or anything. Why the same equipment?"

Mattieu was flicking through the notebook, "Let's assume the worst in this situation. These are two individual members of the CRU. They were sent to scout the area and record what they found. They were left with basic equipment but no provisions. That means that they were meant to forage for their own food, or there is another camp not far from here where said provisions are being held. This could also mean that these two were to relay information over to another camp closer to Kansas City, possibly with those provisions. They could potentially receive information from another camp, somewhere farther west and relay it to the east." Mattieu slowly stood to his full, unimpressive height. "Or it could simply mean that these two were travellers who met an unfortunate end. There really isn't enough here to make assumptions off of."

"Not necessarily," I replied flipping through the note-filled notebook. It had plan designs, layouts of known Kansas City populations, weapons data. The city looked like an olykoek, each section labeled as if it was divided into different counties.

"I do divine," Mattieu said, his eyes becoming wide. "They really had a good bead on us. This is certainly troubling to find, and so early on in our expedition. There's really something off about these people. Something iatrogenic for sure."

I shrugged, "Not sure what else it could be. There really is no explanation for this. It's terrorism all over again, but we're also being terrorized by the contaminated."

"Life's tough," Mattieu replied. "The good lord will make sure we will be okay, however that may be."

"Didn't take you for the religious type."

"Just because I don't go thrusting it in your face doesn't mean that there isn't something special up above."

"Woah," I backpedaled a bit. "I'm not judging, you just caught me a bit off guard is all."

Mattieu smiled, "Faith has pushed me this far along, and I'd like to see how much farther I can go before I go home to my wife and daughter."

"Do you really think it's possible?"

"Possibility isn't the question, Zach."

I breathed deep before exhaling slowly. "Sorry. I guess seeing these bodies has made me all sentimental and whatnot. I don't mean to bring the mood down."

"Nonsense," Mattieu said, waving me off. "If there is ever a need to talk, even for me to just sit with you and let you ramble, I'll be more than happy to do that. What you say stays with me."

"Thanks, Mattieu."

Suddenly, without warning, pops were heard in the distance, sounding like blunt firecrackers. "Someone's shooting!" I shouted at Matthieu. We ran outside, quickly mounting up.

"AH!" Mattieu shouted, grabbing his lower back. "Go! I'll catch up." I stared at him, waiting for some miracle back pain remedy. "GO!" he shouted, pushing my horse forward.

My steed started at a quick trot. I didn't know where I was going, admittedly, but it couldn't be far. The pops of gunfire were getting louder, but were further separated between each shot. The heels of my boot dug into the horse's sides, spurring him on. The hooves clattered against the pavement faster and faster until the sound became one constant blur.

They must have found someone, hopefully. The shots were firing in all directions, two groups trading volleys of bullets. All of the noise was bound to attract unwanted attention.

The rifle strapped to my back was instantly in my hands. It was a bolt action rifle for distance. The automatic was at my horse's side. If we came upon a contaminated, I wanted to be sure to get a clean shot at a distance, hence the rifle on my back.

Pulling hard on the reins, my horse made a hard left turn, away from the action. I was no doubt perpendicular to the blaze of bullets and wanted to leave it that way. No reason to get caught in the crossfire. A right hand turn, followed by a quick left. This opened up the roadway to a two laned no-man's land. I pulled my horse to a stop, tying him up to a lamp post.

I poked my head around the corner of a brick building. Two dark shapes were a few blocks down the roadway, taking cover behind buildings on opposite sides of the street. Both had their backs pinned to the building walls, sidearms being drawn in each hand. As they turned around the corner to shoot a volley of lead at my allies, I took the opportunity to run across the street, taking up position behind a tree growing through the sidewalk.

My belly pressed flat against the concrete, elbows supporting the entirety of my weight. The scope pulled up to my eye, crosshairs coming into view. The farther of the two men was a woman. Her hair was pulled tight in a brown bun. She was on the shorter side, with a somewhat hefty build. Her long black coat flipped and turned in the icy wind. Her companion was a tall man with a dark beanie covering his head coupled with an impressive beard.

The woman was my target, sights quickly fixed on her resting body. She released another volley at Chelsea and Serge, two shots downfield in an instant. Okay - look - I don't generally impress myself with my own shots, but this was a work of beauty, some Shakespear kind of shit right here, though far bloodier and less romantic. I pulled the trigger after the woman's second shot, right as she thought that safety was right around the corner. Instead, she received a three inch hole through her skull, plastering the 'safe wall' with her inner debris.

Her partner cursed loudly, shouting something inaudible. He was looking left, then right, wondering if he should keep fighting or give up and run. But running wasn't an option. Before he had a chance to move, a bullet passed through his knee, crippling the man. He fell to all fours. Defeated, the man tossed his weapon out in front of him, conforming to a full surrender.

I gave myself a small whoop of victory before standing to my full height. Chelsea and Serge must have been approaching the fallen man as his hands were raised over his head and he looked right down the road they were approaching from. I crossed the street to where my horse was desperate to flee from his bonds. Holding firm to the reins, I untied my steed and mounted him, calming it down with a quick pat.

There was a large dumpster that crashed into the corner of the street where my horse was standing, forcing me to make a wide turn around. But before I came into full view, I froze. Six bodies were standing around the fallen man, each looking down onto him. I quietly dismounted, pulling my horse's head low to hide behind the dumpster as much as it could. I pulled out the scope, aiming it at the face of one of the cult members. He had a bloody mouth, a patched cloak covering most of his body, and a contaminated at his side. CRU.

Did I take the wrong side in that firefight?

I felt sick, vomit worthy. I just murdered a woman and crippled a man who may have had nothing to do with this. I knew nothing about them but assumed, and killed. Fuck. This whole time I thought that I was helping, but-

POP! A gunshot sounded. The man that I crippled was no longer moving.

My chest sank. I thought my heart stopped moving for a second. I'm a murderer. My grip twisted on the rifle. I was going to take out as many of these madmen as I possibly could. The contaminated was already tearing at the fallen man's body, another off to the side defiling the woman.

Hot wetness draped down my cheek, falling along all of its ripples just to freeze on the cold hardened pavement below. My finger steadied. A deep breath. Tip of the finger pressed against the curve of the trigger. I'm a murderer now. I'll murder my enemies as well. It was too easy.

A gentle hand caressed my shoulder. A wave of warmth

flowed over me. Another hand calmly cupped my trigger finger, loosely pulling it off and away. Chelsea turned me towards her, her soft eyes calm, comforting to my own. She leaned forward and kissed me, pulling me into a full hug. After a few seconds, she pulled back, signaling for us to leave quietly.

Serge and Mattieu were waiting at the next corner, quietly signaling to walk with the horses away from the CRU members.

Chelsea never gave that rifle back to me.

CHAPTER 7 - RED

"In," the female voice said as she nudged me forward with her rifle. The weapon was in one hand while Mary's reins had to have been in the other as her consistent clopping followed me along the paths. Mary apparently had a new allegiance now. Traitorous pirate horse.

I pushed through the threshold, stumbling on the lip to the entranceway due to the blinding blindfolds my captor fastened around my head. I walked through and into a stifling hallway. The walls were tight, so tight I could hear her struggling to pull Mary in with us. The horse whinnied and moaned, but eventually gave in. The tip of the rifle jabbed into my upper back again, nudging me onward. My hands, outstretched, eventually came into contact with another door at the end of the hallway. *So we're in an apartment, probably.*

I opened the door without difficulty, being an expert at opening unlocked doors for approximately fifteen of my twenty years of existence. As soon as I stepped in, the woman pushed my shoulder, throwing me down to the side. I heard her guide Mary into the room.

"You can take off the blindfold," her hard voice called.

I pulled back the fabric over the eyes. Light rushed at me, causing me to squint. I saw the woman, my captor standing next to Mary. She was loosening the buckles and straps holding the saddle in place before pulling it off entirely.

My eyes finally came into focus. The girl - or woman - had dark orange, almost brown, hair in waves and curls extending down to her shoulder blades. She had icy blue eyes and cliche pale skin dotted with freckles. Her body was hidden behind her winter garb, but the long legs brought her up to Mary's shoulder height.

Before I could speak, the woman raised the rifle, pointing it directly at my chest. "Don't even think of pulling something. I will shoot you without hesitation."

I was sitting straight up now, my hands perfectly still at my sides. None of my weapons were with me. She took them immediately after the capture. I missed Milly.

She reached around a corner and pulled out a wooden chair. "Sit."

"But there's no cushion," I managed to get out before she pushed me hard into the seat. I landed with a painful thud. "Sitting."

"Hands behind your back," she said, holding up a pair of handcuffs.

My hands raised instinctively over my head, "Not into that, sorry. Really though, I can't deal with my hands tied up."

"I will shoot you."

"Look," I started as I shifted my hands behind my back. "I'm just passing through - looking to meet someone in Denver and be on my way. Keep Mary and I'll be off without a word."

"Who's Mary?" She looked over at the horse. "Oh you are a sorry soul. Cuff yourself, please."

"Can you show me that you do have the key? I might go into a panic attack if I am tied up without a way to be freed."

She pulled a jingling key ring out of her pocket, clashing the gold and silver keys together. "Cuffs. Now." She loosely tossed the handcuffs at me. I had no choice but to clip them together. I did so, leaving them loose enough to avoid chafing on my wrists.

"Thanks," she said. A weight in her stern shoulders loosened, giving her a more relaxed look. "Now, I'm also waiting on someone. Therefore, you best start by telling me your full name."

I hesitated for a moment. Giving something in me wanted to lie about who I am, to keep my identity a secret. What if this girl was a member of the CRU who learned about me after the MA-L incident. Then again, what if she was looking for someone entirely different from myself or a CRU freak. "Darryl Willows."

"And who are you looking for?"

"That's a good question," they didn't tell me, though if this was ZmB1EtR, then they knew that. "The only way I know them by is ZmB1EtR."

"Oh," her eyes went wide. "So is there anything else I should know about you or your mystery friend, Darryl Willows? Are you with others?"

"No."

"How long have you been on your own?"

"I've lost track. A while?"

"See? This is the problem I'm having. There's absolutely no way to identify you to not be a part of the CRU. What can you prove to me?"

I chuckled. I'd found who I was looking for. "The only place anyone called them the CRU was on the forum where we met. How's it going, ZmB1EtR?"

"Jesus cracker! You scared the hell out of me, Darryl. What were you doing, roaming around Denver like that?"

I metaphorically shrugged my arms, "What was I supposed to do? I couldn't text you. You never gave me your phone number."

She smiled, revealing teeth undoubtedly formed straight by braces. "Took you long enough to get here."

"I had some company on the way. That's how I jacked Mary."

"I can't believe you named your horse Mary."

"After the pirate? C'mon Mary Read? You don't know of her?"

She shook her head, "Never heard of such a salty horse."

An awkward silence followed. For all of the time that I had chatted with her online, I had no idea what to say next. My eyes looked the woman up and down, letting them linger only when she looked awkwardly to the side. "So do you have a name? Or should I call you Gingie?" I asked after a minute of dead silence and misconstrued eye contact.

She blushed a bit, her freckles hiding behind the crimson glow of her cheeks. "Red."

"Red? Like the dad from 'That 70's Show'?"

She shook her head violently, "No, my parents thought it would be ironic as I came out with a full head of fluffy red hair. They are no longer around to be ironic," she said as her voice trailed off. Red walked around in a circle, nervously pacing about.

"What's up, Red?"

"You can call me whatever you'd like. I know that you were with Chelsea, which is a normal name. So call me whatever. I'd rather not have awkward moments. I don't even know why I told you that. I should have made something up. Now -"

"Relax, Red. I think it's a good name. Certainly fits you, and not just because of the hair," I shifted in my cuffs. They were loose on my wrists but were starting to chafe regardless. "As my old friend, Zack, would say: in some automatical way, I really think it fits."

Before I knew what happened, the rifle was pointed back at me. The barrel was directly against my nose, and I had to sneeze. "Speaking of, where is Chelsea?" Red asked maliciously.

I was beginning to sweat now. Being interrogated at gunpoint really has no positive for the interrogated individual. "She's in a safe zone," I replied. "Along with my aforementioned friend, Zack. You probably know him as Buffalant99. He found us, though some way online, in Jersey and we travelled together."

"So why aren't you in that safe zone with them?" Red asked, not buying into my story.

"Please put the gun down. I'm clearly tied up and not moving anywhere. It would make it a ton easier to not directly fear being shot while speaking." Red lowered the weapon, only to have it aim at a larger target which I shall not give further description. "The safe zone is in Kansas City. Zack found it to be a powered zone at the very least. Where we were holed up was becoming overrun with the contaminated. Regardless of it being a real safe zone or not, we had to move and take a chance. I don't know if you remember him, but we had a guy on the forum who lived in Illinois. He was supposed to meet us on the way. Turns out the freak belonged to the CRU and was trying to infiltrate the safe zone. If you pull back the collar of my jacket, you'll understand why I didn't accompany my friends to the safe zone."

Red slowly walked behind me, lifting back my jacket to see the deep red bubbly scar formed from when I was bitten. I felt her colt fingers roll across each peak and valley, lingering where the damaged flesh sealed up against healthy skin. I heard a quick clank followed by a twist. The cold steel which bound my hands was no longer attached. Red made a supererlogatory motion by loosely rubbing the marks left behind by the cuffs.

"Thanks," I said, rubbing my hands out of habit. "Though I'm a little surprised that you trust me enough to let me loose."

She shrugged, tussles of golden-red hair jostling with the motion. "There's a scar, and something like that doesn't heal overnight. That's a nasty bite right there, no doubt. Probably took a while for it to simply scab up, let alone seal again. Contamination takes approximately three days to fully set in, the likes of which that wound would not have healed during. Therefore, you're either the cure or got lucky."

Not bad. "I'm not the only one. Chelsea got lucky as well. No idea why. Maybe we're just immune to the disease."

"I don't think so. If you were, I feel like there would be others which has gone widely unreported."

"Reports really aren't a big thing nowadays."

"Hilarious," Red said. She placed her rifle down in the corner of the room. Mary gave a light pant, coaxing Red to come over and stroke her mane. "Rest for tonight. There's no reason to worry. We're safe enough here in the Denver wild."

"About that," I started. I was standing now, eyeing up the rifle. "I had some CRU following me here." Red quickly looked over to my, her head twisting at an awkward angle. "They've been following me for a few hundred miles, actually. I kind of pissed them off when I stole Mary and shot one of them."

Red quickly moved to the rifle, "Where were they located, and how many?"

"I found them collaborating in a church in a small town called Stratton. Honestly, I'm not so sure how many there were.

Enough to make me flee like a bat out of hell. If I had to guess, I would say probably ten or so in the church with half of that following me. But be warned, these guys had some weird alliance with the contaminated."

"Alliance?"

"Something along those lines. I saw some bitch drinking contaminated blood, but the ritual was different than other induction ceremonies I've seen for the CRU. This was more of a power evolution than their normal - turn into a contaminated - evolution." My mouth was beginning to dry out with this talk. Every moment I spoke, the CRU gained ground on my position. "We're in danger here."

Red looked down the scope of her rifle, wiped a piece of dust away, quickly flared back the bolt to load a round in the chamber, then said, "We're good. Let's go hunting."

She was calm as we walked silently down the streets of Denver. Red reached a building and, without hesitation, walked through its shattered glass door towards the interior stairs. The building was large, larger than I was suburbanly used to. Though I lived quite close to a very large city, I never really explored it on my own, always being too intimidated by the scale of everything.

Red was fearless. She marched without pause up to the eighth floor. In a past life, I'd be strongly panting at this point. However, due to the contamination, Red and I did not need a rest to catch our breath.

A shattered window let in the cool winter breeze. Red went right up to it, pointing out the window with the nose of the rifle. She had her eye lined up with the scope, long curled red hair pressed over the front of her head to cancel out any exterior light. "I knew a guy once, a real towser," she said through quiet breaths. "Really wonderful guy. The only thing was that he was a bit of a bitch. Scared easy. When the contamination really took hold, he lost it. Always droning on about how the earth was doomed and humanity is a waste of space. There's no tomorrow blah blah here comes the messiah of death." I heard a quick click of the safety unlocking the trigger mechanism. "The only thing he was right about is that people are dying, and unless we start preserving humanity, then we're ultimately going to wipe each other off the map. These CRU need to be stopped. They are the problem. So let's see what they do when their friend's head bursts like a bloody water balloon."

This chick was weird, but in a good way.

A sharp crack echoed in the small office room followed by Red loading another round into the chamber. "Missed, but we're too far away for them to hear the noise."

"How many?"

"Three on horseback. Two walking. Contaminated I presume?"

"Most likely. Speaking of contaminated, how are the city monsters distributed?"

"No idea," Red replied quickly. Another sharp crack. "Oh they noticed that one. Whizzed by the tall guy's head." Another round. "There's no reason for me to really track the contaminated. I'm fine in my bubble. As long as the bubble isn't overrun, then I'm safe. To be fair, there really aren't a lot of contaminated anyway. If there were, they're all at the football stadium. That's where the refugees were being holed up when this initially went down."

"Same thing happened by me. Except I have no idea what happened to the people in the stadium," I replied, recalling the dangerous adventure Chelsea, Zack and I had at Metlife Stadium.

"Neither do I," Red replied. "My only guess would be that they were moved to another safe zone, similar to your Kansas City. If not, then everyone who went there is probably dead or turned." Another crack, "Got one!"

I stared out the window. There was a clear view of the CRU in the fields approaching Denver. How Red actually made that shot was beyond me as the bullet had to have traveled nearly half a mile. Luck must have played a part. "I'm impressed you found my assailants so quickly," I commented.

"Eucatastrophe," she replied, loading another round into the chamber.

"Euca-what?"

"Eucatastrophe," Red said. She pulled her hair away from the scope, wrapping the curls around the back of her head. "An unexplainable catastrophe which leads to a conclusion. Look, your friends are leaving. Problem solved. Eucatastrophe." Red stood up to her full unimpressive height. "We good?"

I shrugged, "I guess so."

"Let's go back and have some rooftop churrasco."

"Where do you get these terms?"

She actually had a barbeque, a full on propane grill at the roof of the complex. The roof itself was entirely snowcapped, other than a shovel-width path leading to the aforementioned grill.

"The one good thing about winter," she started. "Is that you don't need a freezer to keep things frozen." I kicked aside some snow with my good boots keeping my feet nice and dry. Red started up the grill, clicking three burners on to maximum. Shortly after, heat waves were visible above the stainless steel grill cap. She slapped the meat on the grill, a wave of delicious smelling hisses erupting from beef against hot irons.

"This is pretty nice, what you have up here."

"Thanks," Red replied quietly. "If I managed to make it to the summer, I'd like a wicker couch, maybe a table with an umbrella too. A nice lounge. I could even set up a bar if I managed to find the effort. A garden as well. A garden would be nice to have, growing food would make things so much easier."

"That'll be easier come spring with me around, assuming you plan on keeping me that long. Have you thought about that at all?"

She shrugged, resting her hands against the side of the grill. "Not really, but what are our other options?"

"You could get into Kansas City. It's a bit of a walk, but I made it this far. There's no reason the two of us can't make it back."

"Not sure if I want to do that. Like you said, it's nice up here." Red took tongs and flipped the meat. Another chorus of angry vipers sounded from the grill. "It could be nicer, now that someone else is around."

"Nicer isn't necessarily safer."

"What is really *safe* anymore? Even if we are in Kansas City, even if there is a plethora of military people, even if there is an abundance of crops and cattle, that does not constitute safety. Comfort - maybe - but not safety." Red flicked the meat around a couple of times, inspecting the outside for consistent grill lines before flicking off the burners and slapping the beef down on a plate.

We walked inside in silence, our boots squealing as they grazed against the wooden steps. Red then cut in front of me, pushing her way past and into a side room. I followed her into a seating area, what one might have called a dining room, before the fan was covered in shit. A six foot long rectangle oak dining table was surrounded by six chairs. There were no other furnishings in the room other than a blue paisley vase resting against the far corner nearest the window looking over the front of the building.

"You kill easily," I said as bluntly as possible. Red was in the process of using a very sharp knife to slice the steak into strips. Her pale hands paused for a moment before continuing. "I've never killed a man, as far as I know. Or should I say that I've never really been the aggressor."

"At the church you were."

"This is also true," I stumbled through my words. Did I really think myself better than she? While I wasn't looking for trouble at the church, I certainly found it and acted upon it. I also created the improvised explosive. "Look," I continued. "It's just foreign to me, to see someone attack without seemingly thinking about it."

"Some people have to do what must be done," Red replied, harshly stabbing a corner piece of the beef and loping it into her mouth. "Sometimes you have to do what really doesn't seem like the most humane course of action," she said with a bulge of food hidden in her cheek.

"I've just never seen someone kill like that-"

"Do you think I wanted to kill those people?!" she lashed out angrily, whipping the knife in one clean motion across the room. It flew horizontally into the wall, sticking half way into the sheetrock. "You said that they were after you. You told me that they wanted you dead. What was I supposed to do? Hide? Until they found us and killed us of course! This is no longer a time of trials and tribulations. This isn't a shit-fest of fun-loving terrorism anymore. There is no such thing as 'life,' instead we're stuck in a death world. Individual life is no longer precious; only the individual life is." She sniffled sharply, then wiped an invisible tear off of her cheek. "I don't want to be this way, but it's the only way to survive. Anything else is bullshit or a way to get yourself killed. I finally found someone who might understand this, and I don't want us to get killed."

A silence followed. This world couldn't really be dead, at least not to the point of no return. Right? "My father once said, 'You can't put horns on a sheep.' Then I'd reply: What if you glued them on? 'Well they'd still wash off in the rain. And you are thusly still with a sheep. Just ask your mother.' Followed by a slap by the aforementioned mother." I shifted awkwardly around the table to stand next to Red, facing her icy blue eyes. My hands resting on her shoulders, I turned her to face me in full. "Neither of us wants to be the goat, but right now we need to glue on some horns. And as soon as this is all over, we'll wash them off."

She smiled at me, the pale pink of her lips breaking ever so slightly, "That's a terrible metaphor." Then she laughed, a beautiful deep laugh with all of the color and spirit not found in Kansas anymore Toto. It warmed bones chilled by the frigid winter and thawed the small apartment dining room. Then something took over me. Red's laugh tweedled me in, and I fell for her harpy song. She reached up, placed her hand softly behind my neck and pulled her lips forward onto mine. It was a good kiss, a wonderful sweet song placed onto my mouth all the way from Red's tender touch to the minty taste of the lip balm mixed with campestral fields of steak lightly seasoned in salt and pepper.

I pulled away a moment later, "This doesn't feel right." but it did. The companionship humans so longed for, I so longed for, found me again. So why was I running?

Red shrugged, not mockingly or out of anger, but because

what else could she motion? "You haven't been here long, Daryll, but as I said before, I like you here. I'm sorry you lost Chelsea." Then, as if everything was as normal as before the contamination, Red sat down at her plate, placed a healthy slice of steak on it, and slapped enough steak sauce to change the flavor of her taste buds forever.

She was right, in a way. Chelsea was gone and it was about time I moved on. This life we had now was not one of subtle hints and gestures. Either one of us could be gone tomorrow. And on that ridiculously small chance that I ever found Chelsea again, she wouldn't be the same Chelsea I once knew. At least probably not.

I sat down at the table. We ate in silence.

Red disappeared into the kitchen without a word. After a short clank of glass, she re-emerged with two drink glasses, each a quarter full. "Do you like scotch?"

My stomach churned, "I haven't had it in a while, only once when I was nineteen. Needless to say, I didn't have much of a taste for it back then."

She shrugged, "You're older and more experienced now. Scotch is a drink that gets better with age." I took the glass and immediately downed half the drink. A fire erupted as the scotch crawled down my throat, finally subsiding to a warm belly. "It's also a drink that demands respect," she added, noticing the subtle tears welling up in my eyes. Red took my hand and led me into the living room. There was naught but an inactive brick fireplace and two long paisley couches atop a bland shag rug. The hardwood floor creaked with each of our steps. "Shoes off," she said.

I shrugged, not thinking twice while still holding the half of a half glass of scotch in my hand. I kicked my good boots into the corner of the room and flopped down on the couch closest to the fireplace. Red began to start a fire. "Don't worry," she said. These logs burn clear enough so that nobody will notice the smoke. I sniffed the scotch, sweet smoky flames shooting up my nose. My corrupted mind had to convince the rest of me to take another sip. This time the rush of alcohol was not as harsh. Either I was getting used to the drink, or it was already affecting me.

"So what's your plan?" Red asked as she sat down on the couch opposite me. She was laying Roman-style on the couch, fully sprawled along its full length.

"What do you mean by that? My plan was to come here."

She scoffed, "Well now that you are, in fact, here. Thusly leaving you without a current plan, so what is it?"

A small bulge was protruding from the hip of her yoga pants. Red was armed. "My plan?" I started, taking another sip of scotch. It went down easier with each taste. "I am a bit arrears, one might say. My plan itself is simply to survive, which I have been doing quite fine on my own so far. I wanted to survive with Chelsea, move forward with our lives as the couple who survived being spit on by hell to come out of it together. Unfortunately hell got me pretty good, right in the neck." I finished the scotch, but Red refilled it before I could rest the glass on my leg.

She was screwing the top back on with her back to me. I quickly did a wrap around, grabbing Red at the waist with one hand and pulling the revolver from her back with the other, all without spilling a single drop of scotch.

"I don't enjoy being interrogated while at gunpoint."

Red launched herself from my grip, rocketing back to the couch. "What? You really don't trust me? Who says I couldn't have shot you earlier if I really wanted to."

I shrugged, "You could have, but now I have the leverage. No more getting me drunk to interrogate me, to see what I may or may not say." I finished the scotch in one quick gulp. My stomach roared with anger as it went down.

Red looked to be on the verge of tears, "You really take me for a threat? Do you really not get it, Darryl?" She stood now, slowly pacing towards me. I held the gun out as if I was really going to shoot her. "I'm tired of being alone, Darryl. I'm tired of hiding. I'm tired of living in the ever present fear with death waiting around every corner just to scare the living shit out of me, then watching as He decides not to kill me but instead torture me with a fear of living." Red reached up, wrapping her pale hands around the barrel of the handgun. "If I can't live here with someone who makes me less afraid, then do me a favor," she said, gently placing her forehead on the kill end of the six-shooter. "I'm too tired to do this anymore."

She wanted someone to be with, someone to keep her company. I felt like such a shit-bag right then. But in the back of my mind, a warning kept tingling. This all could have been a ruse, a way to get me to lower my guard and make a meal out of me for some insane CRU ritual. Sometimes you just have to take a leap of faith.

"I'm sorry," I said, slowly placing the gun on the ground and replacing its place in my hand with the scotch bottle Red dropped. "I guess if we're going to be working together, trust has to start somewhere." I picked up her glass, which had also fallen, and refilled it. "We should toast to something."

She raised her eyebrows. There Was no smile on her lips. "What do we toast to?"

"To our survival, duh," I said, pouring scotch into a glass of my own. I was reaching in to clash glasses, but she stopped me.

"We toast to each other," Red said. "We toast to our inevitable longevity in each other's company."

"And the death of our enemies!"

She smiled, finally. "And the death of our enemies!" Before I could add anymore, she clanked her glass against mine and drank.

The scent of alcohol was fresh on her breath as she reached in and kissed me. Her lips parted mine, pushing against my mouth until I kissed back. The room swirled around me in a warm dance. Nothing mattered anymore, just the two of us, Red and I, kissing in the middle of some random apartment on a shag rug between two loathsome couches. And it was amazing, arguably the best kiss I've had, the best since-

I pulled back a bit too quickly.

"Sorry," Red said with a sympathetic smile. "I guess it's a bit too soon, still." She reached up and kissed me on the cheek. "I'll see you in the morning."

Red turned to go but I stopped her. We did nothing wrong. There's no reason to apologize for not doing anything wrong.

Right then I should have pulled her to me, brought Red over to reassure her that everything would be better now, that it will be okay. Then I should have kissed her straight on the lips in a cliche tight embrace, but all I could do was say, "Good night." She smiled, though, a slight edge-of-the-mouth smile before turning around and walking away, her light footsteps echoing in the empty hall.

CHAPTER 8 - AMBUSH

We awoke the next morning, Red about a half hour before me, and there was a silence about the apartment complex. The silence didn't even keep there but stemmed from the whole city. I've never been in such a lively place that was so dead.

A generous helping of bacon and eggs with caramelized onions were on the menu for breakfast. Red chopped everything up but I insisted on cooking, as eggs are one of the few things I am able to successfully cook. We ate as quietly as one might imagine, Red throwing in a nod of approval whenever she moved from eggs to bacon to a combination of the two and onions added on top.

I wanted to talk about our plans, about the megillah that was the CRU, and overall, what *she* wanted to do. There seemingly was just no way for me to come out and say it without forcing myself.

"I'm going on a hunt," Red said a short while after breakfast. Our stomachs were still full, and I was even enjoying my second cup of coffee (this place is great).

"What for?" I asked. It was the first thing I said to her since breakfast.

"Some contaminated. I've been scouting them for quite a while now, learning their patterns, finding the places where they go in and out of the city, where they sleep. Anything that can give me some edge over their masses." Red had her handgun tucked into the back of her pants and was holding a rifle as she checked to make sure the magazine was ready to go. "I'll see you later. Try to stay out of trouble."

"What do you mean? You can't go out there alone?" I said, standing up too fast resulting in the aforementioned second cup of coffee spilling down my pants. "Just let me get my things in order and I'll help-"

"No," Red said. "You stay here. Two of us is too loud. I've been doing this for a while now, and so have you. You should understand the danger of travelling in groups, Darryl." She ran the strap of the rifle around her shoulder, "I'll be back in a couple of hours. Just relax, have another cup of coffee, and enjoy yourself." She came over to me and placed a quick kiss on my forehead as if it was meant to glue me to the spot. Red gave a slight wave and walked out. I didn't even hear the door close behind her.

I looked around the desolate room. There was nothing of relative interest to report. The same two couches and the same shag rug remained. My coffee was finished after a few short minutes, resulting in having absolutely nothing to do in the immediate area. I returned to the kitchen to be greeted by a cooling coffee pot. It was glass with a filter, a pre-electricity coffee pot perfect for post apocalyptic situations. A dribble of condensation had leaked around the side and fell into the burner below.

After a quick refill of my cup (no milk as cows are no longer common and I'll be contaminated before I use that powdered creamer crap), I began venturing through the rest of the apartment building. It wasn't large for an apartment building. I counted four stories high and a basement level. Mary was hanging out on the first floor as she was not very nimble when it came to tight corners as I found out, thinking it would be fun to ride her to the building roof.

Eventually, with yet another steaming cup of coffee in tow, I entered a small studio apartment. It was small, to be frank (and I'm Darryl)(gotta stop talking to you like that, it's draining). The room consisted of a mere desk, second hand used couch from the Eighties, and a bookshelf, each shelf filled with an assortment of colored book bindings.

I flipped through the novels in alphabetical order but found nothing of interest. I finally popped out the Lord of the Rings: The Two Towers and began reading through. It was gripping enough, reading about the constant bout of man vs. walking (really though, the most entertained I've ever been reading about a pack just moving), but I was soon becoming fidgety. My joints were stiffening and my muscles drained from lack of movement. I'd been on the run/horse for the past few months, a sudden halt to that could take a toll for the worse. Endurance was one of the selling points and survival skills humans had left in their arsenal. That and some guns.

Red warned me against it, but there was no way I could stay here much longer without losing myself. My life was an entire bucket filled with danger. Being weary was now something that came naturally to me, possibly the only reason that I'm still alive. Those who are careless and complacent are not around for very long, but here I am. I appreciate Red's warning, but she needs to understand that I'm no damsel in distress.

"Just a quick exploration, maybe a block or two, enough to get the old legs stretched," I said to Chetty as I pushed her into the leather sheath and slapped her on my back. Milly was already comfortable in my pants.

I opened the door slowly, as any cautious adventurer would do. A giant gust of frigid air blew at me, pressing the door open and nearly flinging it off of its hinges. It got in two loud clashes of door handle against wall before I caught it.

The street was very empty, only a couple of snow drifts smashing against the buildings not allowing them to drift further. A couple of hoofprints lined the sidewalk. Red was headed east. A part of me wanted to turn west and follow my own path, another - caring - side of me wanted to head in her direction.

I started west. The apartment was located close to the end of the block. I kept telling myself to just turn around at the next corner. Even if I did run into Red, I just wanted to go around the block for a walk - which was partially true.

My pace was brisk. The winter air was as cold as ever, yet thinner a mile up which made it much harder to breathe. I wondered how the contaminated fared up here - if the thinner air affected them in some way.

The opportunity to test my theory was standing right in front of me at the far street corner. A contaminated stood, half hunched over, with ripped jeans and the semblance of a white t-shirt. It became alerted to my presence, yellow eyes bearing down on me. White crusted drool clung frozen to its cheeks. A hint of red along the outskirts of the contaminated's mouth hinted at a recent kill. The monster began salivating for a meal, a heaping helping of man meat (remind me to edit that out in the rewrite).

"Clank clank," I said as Chetty was drawn from her sheathe. I knocked the dull end of her against the building to my side. This one was fresh, healthy, and ready to go. The contaminated standing before me would allow me to test the actual capacity of the thinner air on the contaminated's altered bodies.

It lunged forward, nearly sliding on the snowy sidewalk. It was certainly at full strength, long strides with high steps which would have made any NFL running back proud. It hissed and growled with each passing stride. I waited until the contaminated was half a block away before turning back down from where I came at a light jog. I had confidence that I was faster, even in my kick-ass boots, but I didn't want to let the contaminated too close.

It turned the corner and I ran. This one was fast which was another indication of a well fed contaminated. My mind faltered for a second, thoughts leading to Red as the possible victim. But she was with Mary, there's no way that Red would have been overtaken.

The contaminated ran as fast as ever, the cold Colorado air didn't seem to slow it down. It then hit me that the contaminated diet constituted quite a large amount of blood which surely provided enough nutrients to keep the contaminated blood rich in oxygen - a theory as to why their superheated bodies were able to survive instead of imploding on itself.

My experiment was over. I planned on a weakened contaminated to chase me. This one was strong, and a threat close to home. The clouds above were thick and opacus, darkening the quiet city. I turned the corner and stood in wait, but before I could ready my stance, a whinny cried out from behind me.

I turned around and saw Mary fleeing from a small wave of contaminated. Red was nowhere to be seen, though her rifle was still strapped to Mary's saddle. Before I had time to wrangle her, the horse flew past and continued down the street. The contaminated lunged from around the corner. Its intended target was Mary, but it missed, instead having a snogging session with the cold steel lamp post. I didn't hesitate. I slammed Chetty directly through the top of the contaminated's head, slicing a piece of dome clean off like half a cantaloupe.

Red jumped out from the far side of the street. She had a pipe in hand, swinging wildly as she backtracked around the building. Her eyes made quick contact with mine before darting back in front of her. Red whipped her arm around then crouched in a spin. The dense pipe smashed against the approaching contamianted's shin, shattering it. The contaminated fell to the ground in a heap but continued to move forward.

Contaminated are not affected by the loss of limb or bone as man is. Though the bone was broken in numerous places, the parasite-virus is still able to manipulate the muscles to strengthen or loosen based on need. This one was able to hold itself up, even after falling, sending sensors to move the muscles as needed.

It didn't make it very far. Red lunged forward with a mighty strike, smashing the pipe into the contaminated's skull. Part of the cap flew off with the attack, flesh covering rotten bone flailing wildly through the winter air. Red smacked down on the contaminated again to make sure it wasn't going to move.

She took a quick step towards me before taking off in the other direction. Before I could call out, three more contaminated jumped out from where she came. They blindly followed her down the path she was going, arms flailing in a hunger filled rage.

I bolted after them, my steps silenced by the surplus of snow on the sidewalk. Red was around the far corner of the block before I managed a few feet. Instead of following, I took off down the street where they all came from. If Red saw me, then there was a good chance that she would eventually turn in my direction for support. If not, she was just being stubborn.

I booked it to the end of the street, though Red was nowhere to be seen. She was probably faster than I, especially with me running in these weighted boots. I pulled out Milly in one hand with Chetty in the other. Red had to be approaching at one point, but she was really taking her time.

It then occured to my dumb ass that maybe she fell or was injured. Before I had another thought, I bolted forward. Red was around the corner, she had to be. If she fell and was bit, I'd do her the honor of putting her away; she didn't need to become one of the contaminated too.

I'd been standing for what seemed like hours at that corner. I wanted to shout, but that would have been a very bad idea. The slightest sound or twitch of movement made me jump in that direction.

I had to go. I had to go find her now. It was too long, too long since I last heard from her. Red, "RED!" I bolted. Forward running wildly as fast as my legs would move. "Red!" Where was she? The street she went down was empty, save a small splatter of blood - still warm. A few drips indicated she ran through an alleyway north of me. "Red." I followed the trail, an opening leading to a wide street, a main strip. Both directions were empty. She had to be near. A hand, a hand was poking out from behind a dumpster. Blotches of red littered the ground, staining the snow drifts around it. I reached it in a moment. The body of a bloodied and battered contaminated lay with its head resting against the dumpster. "Red," this was a good sign. "You're still somewhere. I'll find you."

Something hissed followed up with a gargled cry. It couldn't have been more than a block over. I ran. My legs kicked up snow as my good boots plowed through the sidewalk. The growl hissed again, this time followed by a pang of metal. I ripped around the corner to see Red, her hair splashed with blood as well as her clothes dripping from the carnage.

She threw off her coat, soaked and ruined from the attack. I didn't wait another moment. Before Red could protest, I ran up and embraced her. "What are you doing?" she asked, but not angrily.

I only knew her for a day, maybe a little more, "I needed this." She was right before me, the only social interaction I had. The only person who didn't want to kill me...probably. "I'm sorry I didn't come faster."

"Daryll, you idiot," Red replied. "I told you to stay inside. I can handle myself out here," she said in my muffled hug, though she didn't protest it.

I held her at arm's length, staring directly into her eyes, "We don't need to be a solo project anymore. We're a band now, Red."

"Terrible, terrible metaphor, Daryll," she said with a smile. "However, I was beginning to feel the same way. I was ambushed, Daryll. These contaminated came at me when I was making my basic perimeter rounds. I do it all of the time, scout around three blocks wide along three different routes, all rotating patterns."

"It was an ambush. The contaminated set it up, possibly. Unless those guys I found commanded them to. I'm still not sure how that really works, though. The CRU didn't take the time to explain things to me. The jerks decided to shoot instead."

"Hilarious," Red countered. "Did you see Mary? I jumped off her to fight the contaminated."

"As a matter of fact, I did. She's back by the apartment," I said. "Stay close."

"Don't tell me what to do."

We made our way carefully back the way we came, down the bloodied streets with kicked aside snow drifts and stores with shattered windows.

Red grabbed the back of my hoodie and pulled me into a store. She placed a finger on my lips then pulled me behind the checkout counter. The store just happened to be a liquor store, bottles and bottles of different assorted wines from all over the world lined the shelves. The whisky and scotch shelf at the top behind the counter was nearly empty. Red pulled a small pint bottle of dark gold whiskey off the shelf. She cracked open the twist off top and lifted it to her lips. Without so much as a hiccup or cough she downed two thick gulps of whiskey before offering me the bottle.

I raised my hands as it say 'what?' but she just nudged the bottle farther into my grasp. Not bothering with the thought of an argument, I took a swash and fought the urge to cough it up.

There was a sudden movement from outside the liquor store. The clops of multiple horse's hooves followed closely by the jangling chains of individuals dismounting their steeds. The people were talking in hushed voices, so low that I could hear Red taking another drink over the sound of their voices.

"Then find her!" a voice lashed out over the common silence. "If you think that the girl really got away from your ambush, then maybe you should be the one hidden in the alleyways with our brethren, all of whom have made a greater sacrifice than you have bothered with, Marvin." The voice was harsh, a cold hardened pitch of a woman with a throat bogged down by too many cigarettes.

"With respect, my lady, you have only just attained the voice," Marvin replied.

It suddenly hit me. This was Marvin, *the Marvin,* the one who had knocked me out and left me to become food as a first 'blessing.' The voice was the exact same, arrogant but knowledgeable. A know-it-all who generally knew what they were talking about. It took a lot within me to not reach above the counter to have him reconcile with Milly.

The other speaker whipped around. Her image, while distorted, was visible to me in the reflection of a clear whipped cream vodka bottle resting above the register. She threw around her bright red cloak as she inaudibly hissed at Marvin.

"Ma'am, the woman with the Red hair really isn't much of a threat," Marvin said. "She's good with a rifle, I'll admit, but she is only one person."

"Now a second has joined her," the woman in charge said. "These are the two we were supposed to use for the ritual through our online friend. We had a plant, and someone didn't follow the rules. Your ambush in Missouri screwed up catching them and your ambush in Denver has gone awry. Your ability may just be in question, Marvin, after all of these blunders. I do not know how long they will be tolerated."

"I have done nothing but serve this cause," Marvin countered. His voice was becoming shaky but the rage behind it was more sure footed. "I have done everything in my power to fortify the backbone of the organization in better service of the Lords above. Neither my integrity nor contributions to this principle shall be in question, just as they never have been."

"Best they stay that way, Marvin, else the Lords above may have something in your destiny," she replied. Her reflection showed the woman swirling her cloak around once more. "Ah," she said. "Maybe it's time for a drink? The lords have pointed us directly at the lovely liquor store. Come, Marvin. You two wait here."

Red's eyes went wide once the boots of our enemies sounded against the wooden floorboards. I grabbed the back of Red's head and pushed her down. The air was cold and our breaths were smoky. There was no way that I'd be caught by these CRU pretending to be a kid smoking a cigarette with my breath. The door loosely shut behind them, bell ringing as the door closed.

"You vilipend me, Marsha," Marvin said after he was sure that the door was fully closed. "What is worse - you do it in front of my subordinates. If you have an issue with me, take it up with me. This blatant ranting in an effort to push me down is in no way unifying our cause."

Marsha was clanking between bottles of wine. "Ah! A very dark cabernet all the way from lovely California. So many of the wine connoisseurs will tell you that the best wine comes from France or Italy, however, I've really acquired a lovely taste for the very rich and dry California grapes." There was a short pause followed by a cork popping from the bottle. "Now come, share a drink with me, Marvin." Marsha poured two glasses, each resting on the counter above where Red and I were hiding.

"I don't drink," Marvin replied.

"I can't do this alone, my friend."

Marvin scoffed, "Oh, your friend? Maybe I should have a

drink after hearing that blessing." His reflection in a bottle resting on the top shelf confirmed the voice. I could do it now, whip out Chetty and cut right through him, taking down the bastard and the bitch, seemingly two higher ranking members of the CRU. I motioned to Red, but she shook her eyes 'no.'

"It's hard, Marvin, to be a high ranking official in this type of business," Marsha said. "We are under constant pressure to get this thing moving and keep it pressing forward. Without results, we shall lose members of our party, the inevitable result of - well - lack of results."

"Everyone has their limits," Marvin said as he sloshed a sip of wine.

Marsha clinked her glass with his, though Marvin did not extend his as an offer. "The only limits a person has is the limits set within themselves. That's what makes us special, you and I; we know the limits as well as how to surpass them. Instead of going for the gold, we wait, biding our time and improving ourselves with the silver until the gold is surely in reach. Do you understand, Marvin?"

"Your metaphors could use some work (fuck I nearly snorted), but the message is there."

"So you see, when I do these things, go on such triads as those presented a few minutes ago, it is not that I doubt you nor do I harbor any mistrust. The fact of the matter is: we are gold, right now. Our organization and beliefs are growing at an alarming rate. Chicago, Boston, even Washington now follow our cause. Other than Kansas City and select other safe zones, there really is nothing that can stand in our way. The evolution of man is here, my friend, yet the gold is not *our* limit."

"To evolution," Marvin said, extending his glass.

"One second, I need more wine," Marsha replied, hastily pouring a glass. "Ah to hell with it. I'll use the bottle." She ran the bottle of California cabernet sauvignon against the wooden countertop as she went to toast. "To the evolution, and to our success." The bottle clashed against the wooden countertop. "This is good wine. I'm taking the bottle with me," Marsha said, a hint of slur in her voice.

"We should be off," Marvin said. "That girl could still be around, if she hasn't gone into hiding yet. We're tracking where she lives but there really isn't much to go on around here."

"Then let us be off!" Marsha cried in a drunken stupor. The door opened, bells rattling behind as it swung shut.

I lifted Red's chin to my own and kissed her lightly on the lips, "Are you okay?"

"Of course I am," she said. Red's arm was covered in blood from where she killed a contaminated. "I swear that's not my own blood," she said when she caught me looking at her arm.

"C'mon, let's get out of here. I recognized one of those guys, Marvin," I said. Red pecked me on the cheek as we stood up, which certainly surprised me.

"Thanks for coming after me," she said. "Even though you didn't really contribute, and I ran away from you, it's nice to know that someone cares enough to risk themself for me."

"No proble-"

The door bells rang as the wooden half glass door swung open. "Marvin, I just need another bottle of this wine - YOU!" Marsha roared, smashing her bottle of wine against the counter and holding us up with the glass point.

Milly whipped out of my back pocket and Red had the lead pipe drawn a second prior. Marvin appeared on the other side of the other side of the door, a handgun of his own pointed directly at me through the glass. He waved a hand and whilstled. Two more cloaked members with snow covered bandanas hiding their nose down appeared with rifles in tow.

"Daryl?" Marvin questioned. "Wow, can't believe I'm getting this chance. Marsha, he's the one who killed our disciple back in Milwaukee. He was supposed to be her first blessing."

"Right up until I mashed her face in with my boot," I replied.

Marvin nodded, "As much as I enjoy reminiscing about the past, please drop your weapons."

"Please go fuck yourself," Red replied. I've never fallen in love with someone in such a short time, finding it to be impossible to do so, but Red really got me. "If you need help, we can start with this pipe." (<3)

I clicked back Milly's hammer, "As she said. Now, please get out of our way."

Marsha raised the hand holding the wine bottle, "Do not move, Marvin. They may get one of us, but neither of them will make it out alive. That is a fact."

Marvin's weapon did not waiver, "I realize that, however, I would prefer that we all make it out of this alive." Marvin signaled to his men to back up. He held the door behind him as he moved outside. "Marsha, please."

Disgruntled, the woman marched out of the building and onto the street. The group grabbed their horses and crossed to the other side of the road, two car lanes wide.

I exited the building first, being the chivalrous lad that I am. Red was close behind. Marvin began to walk across the street, his horse back with the remainder of the group. Marsha was right behind him, "Stop?" I said holding up Milly. Marvin's hands were in the air but he didn't stop pressing forward. "Really, I'll shoot."

"There's no need to shoot, Darryll," Marvin said. He stood on the double yellow lines, exactly halfway through the street. "Think about it. If I really wanted to, I could simply send an army of our evolved brothers to this very place and have them decimate not only that liquor store, but the entirety of Denver."

"So I should shoot you now, right? Before any of that bad stuff can happen."

He had a smirk on his dark face, not arrogant, but amused. "No, that won't help anything, my friend."

"You're not friends," Red said.

"I'll make you an offer," Marvin continued without acknowledging Red. "I'm giving you the chance, the one time deal to see what kind of people we really are. You are a resourceful individual, Darryll. Of those surviving the evolution, you may just be the most worthy to evolve. Fighting is hard. Join us and let it go. Become part of what the Lords and Ladies above deem fit to continue into the future. Join us, Darryll, and your friend can come too. You both can experience what it is like to really be a part of something special, something sacred, something better than before."

Red spat on the cold pavement, "We'd never do such a thing."

It was an out, a way for Marvin to rid himself of an annoying enemy as well as build a stronger CRU.

"We can make you stronger than you could ever imagine, Darryll," Marvin said. "We can communicate with them, the evolved. They feel our plight. They *feel*, Darryl."

"They feel?" I asked. Marvin nodded, a cold stone stare down acknowledgement of my question. Red looked to me, and I met her stare. The rolling red curls wrapped behind her shoulder blades were glowing in the afternoon light. She shook her head again.

"You have only one option, Darryll," Marvin said. "Regardless of how this encounter resolves, we cannot let you two get out of here. That is the bottom line. So choose: join or die. But remember, Darryll, a person of your caliber can possess the ability to evolve without turning into one of our brothers. You are strong, and will become stronger if you work with us."

"Show me," I said. "I want to see how the contaminated feel."

Red glared at me, her face stern and quickly matching the color of her hair. She looked as if she was about to smash my face in with the pipe, but turned away, her shoulder cold. "On the condition that Red gets to choose her outcome, and regardless of what she picks, is unharmed."

"I can guarantee that provision," Marvin said.

Marsha stepped forward, "Like hell you can. I'm not allowing it. The girl isn't important, neither of them really are. This deal is void."

"That's enough, Marsha," Marvin said. "Hold your tongue for five minutes and we'll have some progress made in this world." He turned to Red, "What is your decision?"

Before Red could answer, a whizzing sound rippled past our

noses and into the brick wall next to where we were standing, causing it to erupt in a pink plume. We immediately turned down the street, but before we could move, one of the armed CRU clutched his stomach and fell to the ground. Marsha and Marvin ran over to the man while the other stood guard. Another shot flew past my eyes and into the brick. Red grabbed me and threw me back into the storefront. Pop shots kept flying down the street to keep us suppressed. These attackers knew what they were doing.

"Get back!" Marvin shouted as I tried to get up. Red held me low to the ground. "Find your way out - it shouldn't be a problem for you. Follow our trail if you can. Meet us up north in Seattle. The needle is where you can find me." I nodded in response then pushed my way back into the liquor store with Red at my side.

The silhouette of the CRU members ran, fleeing with their horses in tow until they could reach a point where it was safe to mount. The injured member was being carried by the other guard. She wasn't moving.

We pressed towards the back of the shop. "We have to get out of here," Red said. "There's a back exit through the storage." She pulled on my arm, leading me through mounds of boxes and cases of booze. We passed by an unstable stack, my arm brushing against it. It crashed down with a distinct pop of glass, flooding the concrete with rivers of bloody wine.

Red reached the back door. She quickly pulled back a latch and twisted open the deadbolt lock. The door burst open, two masked individuals with scarves wrapped around their head. I didn't have time to draw Milly. We were about to run when the entrance door chimed and two more fell in line behind us.

"Hands up."

CHAPTER 9 - TUMBLING DOWN

It took me a while. "I just can't shake what I did."

"Blaming yourself only makes it worse. It's not like you did what you did to hurt others, Zack," Chelsea said. She placed a comforting kiss on my cheek. "It's not as if you haven't killed others for a good reason."

"Those reasons were for self preservation, or in the defense of others," I said. My voice was noticeably slower and self-pitied in the campfire light. Mattieu snored loud enough to wake up the entire western Kansas. "These people were just like us, trying to survive. I can't help but think that they would have joined us, creating allies to expand our little haven."

"Zack," Chelsea started as she placed a hand on my arm. "You mean so much to me. You've been outstanding these past few months, watching over me and talking when I'm not doing so well back in our little haven. You really have become family to me." She shifted closer to me so that we were side by side, each staring into the firelight. "You have been so quiet on these trips. We've crossed at least two hundred miles in the past few days and you've barely said a word. Your eating is atrocious, barely snacking on a few bites per day. We need you strong, Zack."

"I just see them, the head exploding and the man's kneecap flying out," I replied. "It keeps replaying for me. I can't stop it. I don't know how to keep going on."

"You have to keep going on, Zack," she said in a kinder tone than I would have expected. "You are not the only one to have killed. I shot that soldier, blew the fucker's head clean off. I knew him. He smiled at me, and worked patrol until sunset. He showed me the border walls and the reinforcements keeping them in place. But he was a piece of shit CRU, and that's why I killed him. And if the CRU wasn't around, a hell of a lot more people would be around. You did not kill those people, Zach. The CRU did."

I'd heard it before, the whole speech. How it wasn't my fault and I needed to continue on for the greater good. Chelsea tried her best, and I really did appreciate her dedication. But it wasn't working. Serge barely glanced at me when I was in a mood. Not that he didn't care as I constantly overheard him asking for updates from Chelsea, but he wasn't the overly sentimental type. Or maybe he thought Chelsea could pull me out of this funk better than he could. I was too ashamed to talk to Mattieu, not from his lack of offering, but because I couldn't bring myself to face the man. He represented everything I wanted in a father figure from the balding scalp to the back pains. I let the man down. When it came down to it, I pulled the trigger. I am responsible for the deaths of those two innocent travellers. If I don't squeeze the trigger, they are alive - or alive long enough to where we can identify and help. I alone killed those two.

"Tomorrow is another day, sweetie," Chelsea said with a yawn. The fire cackled loudly inside the warehouse causing the aluminum walls to cackle.

"Yes, it is," I replied. I felt as shitty as ever, but I decided to humor her - give her something to work off of so that she could sleep without worry. She didn't reply, her head slumped against my shoulder with the rhythmic breathing of her back being the only motion.

Didn't sleep that night either.

*   *   *   *

*   *   *

"The notebooks, they keep pointing at Denver," Mattieu said. He was piecing through one of the dead girl's notebooks we found, leafing along one page at a time. "A few pages are torn out, I imagine they were messages sent over to their comrades either with scouting information or further orders. The last note reads that they were on their way back to reinforce another division against fighting in the city. Kansas city's operation would probably have been an attack or bust situation."

"Which it was bust," Serge said. "Do that's our only lead? It seems weak. No idea how long ago those women were laying dormant. That information could be as old as anything. I'm thinking we stick to the plan for now, scouring cities and towns for any information possible, Denver being a last stopping point. After that, we turn around and update the folks back home. Votes for?"

Mattieu and Chelsea raised their hands.

"Against?"

No hands were raised.

"Settled," Serge said, giving me a lingering glare.

We started off again, following the ever flat highway. Kansas was flat, and not the greatest place to be when having emotional issues was traveling along said eternally flat roadways. Minds begin to wander and thoughts linger without so much as a passing shrubbery or flake of grass to pass the thoughts by.

"Ahead," Serge called. "Small town straight up. Finally, a goddamn thing to look at in this wasteland."

"What's the call, Adrian?" Chelsea asked.

Serge pivoted on his seat, "You're with me, Chelsea. Zach and Mattieu follow up in the rear. We'll clear the town, being that it should only be a few small houses and dead farmland. Approach slowly. If you hear shots, approach faster. Keep safe."

Chelsea reached over and gave a gentle tug of my hand. I leaned in and gave her a quick kiss before she was off. My old rifle was slung over her shoulder and her own was attached to the saddlebags.

Mattieu and I remained motionless atop our steeds as we watched Serge and Chelsea ride along the horizon. We watched as they rode, what seemed to last forever must have been near a slow 5k. They finally disappeared behind a gas station.

"Guess we should get moving," I said.

Mattieu kicked at his stirrups, his horse arriving next to mine. "We both know why Adrian wanted you with me. Don't beat around the bush, Zach."

I kicked my horse, trotting it forward. "Well I don't really feel like talking."

"They were dead already, Zach," Mattieu said.

"How dare you," I started. "I killed them. That is a fact. My bullets are responsible for innocent deaths. We could have helped them, but instead I'm a murderer." I pulled my horse around to Mattieu. I felt like hitting him, swinging the crowbar attached to my saddle and striking him across the forehead. "I see them at night, Mattieu. I see what I've done to change this world. I'm not a good person, Mattieu. Everyone here is fooled by my appearance of being a nice, calm, mild-mannered boy who just wants to smile. Well it isn't that way. I hate the people of this world. I hate what it has become and what it has turned me into. These people, I see them at night constantly falling in a pool of their own blood. The knees buckling from under him as he waits for the CRU to finish him off. I don't even see my father at night, Mattieu. As he came for me, my own father tried to kill me, I shot him. I don't even think of it. I've been a murderer for far too long. There is nothing left."

"There is something left, Zachary," Mattieu said. "The fact that you care, the fact that your actions haunt you speaks volumes. It isn't as simple as cause and effect. The situation constantly changes. One's ability to keep the status quo is next to impossible."

"That doesn't mean that I should be okay with being a murder."

"And you shouldn't!" He jabbed a finger at me. "There is a significant difference between a man who makes mistakes and a man who learns from them. You probably ended those lives, but what awaited them at the hands of the CRU would have been far worse." He shifted in his seat which made the sun reflect off his head and into my eyes. "The point is that you care, Zach. And we need you here. We *all* want you here, especially Chelsea. This funk of yours is really paining her. She hates seeing you like this. So, I'm going to tell you something that I've never told anyone before: quit your pussy-shittin around and get a move on."

I cracked a smile, an awkward half laugh. That line coming from a man who looked like Santa in the offseason was too much for me. "That's more like it," Mattieu said. Before we could do anything else, distinct pops echoed from the nearby town. "Move!" Mattieu cried, spurring on his horse. We were at a gallop now, horseshoes thudding against the sandy roadway.

The town seemed to never be getting closer, always a flat mile away. "Can you handle this?" Mattieu asked, holding out his rifle. My stomach swelled and crushed back in on itself all at once. My body went cold. The reins were suddenly out of my hands and my body stiff. "Can you handle it, Zach? We need you for this."

I reached out and wrapped my fingers around the barrel. Sudden feeling and warmth returned to my arm. All I could do was nod at Matthieu. I got this. I had to. Serge, Mattieu, Chelsea - they were all relying on me to be a part of the team and to push forward. I couldn't do that through self pity. I need to get up and move forward. That is the only direction with a future. The future doesn't' wait in the past. It sure as shit hides there, but it waits for no one.

Our horses finally came to a halt at the edge of town. 'Nowhere, Kansas' a green aluminum sign read. Serge rode forward with Chelsea at his side. A man was tied behind the horse, his hands wrapped in thick rope as Serge pulled him forward. Chelsea saw me with the rifle and did a quick double take. I gave her a nod.

"Found this shit," Serge said, yanking on the rope. "Says he was jus' relaxing in Nowhere.   I pulled out a map, scanning Kansas for the small town. It couldn't have been inhabited by more than twenty residents when I scanned the horizon. "The town isn't on this map. A town called Edson is nearby from what I can tell, but no Nowhere."

"That's because this small town is Edson," Serge replied. "So that's how I know this jackass is lyin'."

"I swears it," the man said. He was about my height, pencil thin, with thick scruff and a mop of hair. It looked as if he hadn't eaten in months. "I came here to Nowhere. Didn't not see nothing here other than that sign. I've always known this place to be Nowhere, ever since I was a boy."

Serge leapt off his horse, yanked the man forward then thrust him back so hard that he fell onto the dusty road. "You are lying," Serge said. "Do you want to know how I know that you are lying? I am a former resident of this town, Edson. I grew up here before joining the Marines, jackass." The man went fifty shades of pale. "So now tell me what is going on here."

The man stumbled backwards, his feet sliding against the gravel as if they couldn't move fast enough. "Nothing, I swear it. I'm just looking for refuge in this town is all. A place to crash."

"Nobody in their right mind would crash here!" Serge roared. He whipped out his handgun and held it at the man's shoulder. "I'll pop that off if you don't start speaking up."

"Don't hurt me!" it shouted. " I'm just a lowly pawn. A comms man for the evolution."

"CRU," Chelsea said under her breath.

The man was on his knees now. "I was waiting two more days for our contacts in east Kansas, then I was to move on."

"To where?!" Serge interrogated.

"West," the man was in tears. "I was to head west. My partner went ahead to inform our group."

"Where was your group a few days ago?"

"I don't know - I swear on the gods above. My assignment was to sit here until I received notice of our eastern contacts then move west."

"What's your leader's name?" I asked.

The man looked at me, his eyes went wider than I thought to be humanly possible. "No, please don't ask me that. I can't reveal his name. I've said too much already. He knows - he will know. Shoot me, please! He knows what I have done and will kill me himsel-" the man started seizing, convulsing and retracting. His body flailed against the pavement, his head opening numerous wounds from scraping violently against the ground. Then it stopped.

"Went west, he said," Serge said without even a second glance. "West is Denver then Cali. Doubt they went south enough to Vegas, otherwise we could have some fun. Makes the most sense to keep following the highway to Denver and go from there. Nothing pops up there, then we go back, re-supply for a longer journey, and pick a new direction."

"We should probably bury him," Mattieu said, ignoring Serge's plan.

The marine shook his head, "Leave him to the birds. He's nothing more than CRU scum. Let him rot."

Mattieu got off of his horse. "I don't generally disagree with you, Adrian, but that is the difference between them and us. Maybe he is CRU scum, but we are not. I will bury him myself if I have to."

I jumped down as well, "I'll help you."

"Whatever makes you happy, but don't forget that they would never do that for us. We would be food," Serge said. "I'm going to look through my old town to see if there's anything of value left."

"I'll join you," Chelsea said. "Sorry," she whispered to me. "Just not much of a dead body person, but if it was a live one I'd help."

"You just said you'd bury him alive."

She shrugged, giving me a playful smile.

"Meet at the other side of town in thirty minutes," Serge said.

"Give us forty-five. The ground is hard," Mattieu countered.

"Very well."

The grave took nearly a half hour to dig. We had no conventional tools and were forced to use a combination of our knives and hands. The paltry grave was filled shortly after, a mound of dirt along the roadway being the only marker.

Mattieu and I stood looking over the overturned earth. It had been forty minutes. "Ready?" I asked.

"One moment," Mattieu said as he bent down and drew a cross in the loose dirt. "Here lies a man, one of conviction. Whilst he did not know it, in some way, shape, or form, he served the Lord as the Lord willed him to serve. He can rest in the mercy of God, knowing that in his final moments, the Lord brought him home. God bless." He stood up and brushed the dirt off his knees. "And before someone says it, no, I do not think that the CRU would have said something at our funeral. Let's go before Adrian has another hissy."

We met them at the end of town as requested. The saddle bags slightly fuller. Chelsea had a red bladed fire axe attached to her horse and Serge was chewing on an open can of cold beans. Without another word, we headed off into the unknown reaches towards the mountains, the only thing in sight. We were headed for Denver, the only place we knew to move forward into the future, to see what that devil holds.

*   *   *   *

*   *

Denver approached faster than anticipated. We did nothing but travel along the highway, the beat of the horse's hooves pushing us on. There was no fun, no chatter to pass the time. Speaking only seemed to delay the inevitability lying flat ahead: the continuation of the road. The Rockies housed no solace as our eyes were constantly trained upon their snow capped peaks. Countless miles were covered each day, taking only about three days to reach our destination from Edson.

The city approached, first with scattered buildings surrounding the main nucleus, then with towering skyscrapers and shiny pedestals exclaiming to the world man's domination.

"Football stadium just up ahead," Serge said. "Maybe the CRU passes the time playing a bit of good old American football. What's that?" Serge said. he grabbed his rifle and pointed it in the direction of an approaching noise. It sounded as if someone was grinding a crowbar against thick ice. A brown horse with white spots suddenly barrelled through, bolting past our position and down the main street.

"Someone lost their horse?" I asked.

"More like the CRU lost their horse," Chelsea said.

Serge quickly signaled to dismount. "Tie your horses here. We go quietly on foot." The four of us tiptoed down the road in a single file line. Serge held up a hand, holding us back as he poked his head around the building corner perpendicular to the street we were on. He held up four fingers then pointed back down the street. Serge did a quick double take then signaled six people. Before I could react, he grabbed my forearm and pulled me across the other side of the street.

I could see them now. Four members were on one side of the street, two of them with large firearms. The other two had said large arms pointed at them and exited the building they were in, creeping out with weapons of their own raised.

"Which are the good guys?" I whispered to Serge.

"I'm guessing those two," he said. "Those other four are heavily armed, and if what that guy back in Edson said is true, his people would be here." He waived at Chelsea, indicating that the four were our targets if it came to that.

Chelsea waived back, three fingers raised. Serge shook his head, but Chelsea replied with a scrunched face and biting motion. "Contaminated," she whispered then raised four fingers. The four were with contaminated. "CRU," she motioned.

"What are they doing?" I asked Serge. "If they have contaminated backup, what could they possibly be waiting for? Kill them and get it over with." I pulled back the chamber and loaded a bullet. "Unless we stop them from being killed."

Serge nodded his head then signaled for Chelsea and Mattieu to wrap around the other side of the building to form a pincer strike. Chelsea nodded, then wrapped a scarf around her lower face and took off. "I'm making the decision to take out the CRU. If you don't like it, then you can add supporting fire or hold off to the side."

"I'm with you."

Serge gave me the thumbs up, then aimed down the sights of his rifle. He fired off two quick shots, POPOP. Each bullet whizzed between the group, separating the four from the two. He fired again, launching another volley past the CRU. This time, two of the CRU guards standing to the side returned fire, but they couldn't tell where we were shooting from. Serge landed a shot directly into the gut of one of the men. The guard fell over clutching his intestines. The remainder of the CRU rushed over to help and move. I whipped over across the street to find better cover.

The contaminated were gone. The CRU were packing up their things, already mounted their horses, and were bolting off. "Liquor store!" Serge said as he charged forward. I followed directly at his heels, only trailing by a few small steps. We reached the small shop. Serge poked his rifle through the entrance as I covered his six. He pushed through and patted me on the back twice to follow as something shattered in the back room.

"Don't move," Serge said as two sets of feet pushed through. I turned around as Chelsea and Mattieu came in from the storage area. "I'll hold them. Pat'em down," he told me.

I moved forward to the one with orange hair. She dropped the pipe from her hands and pushed on the man next to her to drop his weapon. He was shaking, the guy. His handgun loosely fell from his grip and he turned around. Chelsea's eyes were wide and pale, as if she was about to pass out.

"Chelsea?"

"Darryl?"

Darryl.

CHAPTER 10 - FORWARD

"Darryl?" the dark skinned man pointing his gun at me asked.

I couldn't peel my eyes off of her, Chelsea's striking blue ocean eyes. They had been gone; I lost them. I was dead to her and now here I am, a ghost to my past. I couldn't move, even as I felt a clap on my shoulder and Zach's lost familiar voice behind me. She found me, after all this time being apart, knowing the other has been forever gone. I found the maltese falcon, the only problem is that I wasn't looking for it, and it wasn't looking for me.

"How-" she started. I just shook my head.

"Woahkay, what is going on here?" Red asked.

Zach walked up to her, "Hi, I'm Zach. These two have a history. Let's go somewhere quiet and uncontaminated to let them talk."

"Nu-uh," the military man said. "No way is Chelsea going out of my sights. She's my best shot."

"Again, Adrian, I rarely disagree with you, but this is another of those times," a portly man with a moustache said. He walked over and placed his hands on Adrian's rifle, lowering it. "Let's give them a few. We'll be right outside."

The door closed, the jingling bells signaling their exit.

A pressurized silence surrounded us, pounding on our bodies from all sides but not enough to make us crumble.

"So," she started but couldn't get anywhere.

I walked over to the top shelf and opened a bottle of

whiskey. I poured each of us a glass then downed mine before refilling it.

"Gotta drink to talk to me?" Chelsea asked with a coy smile. She drained her own and signaled for another.

"I don't know how I'm alive," I said. Blunt was always the best way for me to start conversations. "I never really thought about it, but before I knew it, both you and Zach were gone for a week, and I was still here."

"What did you do then?"

I shrugged, "Survived. What anyone else would do. I tracked down some contaminated and killed whichever I could in a petty sense of revenge. They stalked me all the same. It wasn't until I accidentally came into contact with Red that I really had a purpose."

"You didn't want to return to us?" she asked.

"Of course I did, but I didn't see any feasible way to do it."

"I got in."

"Your scar healed better." I pulled back the flap on my jacket, revealing the bubbly tissue from where I was bit. She seethed when looking at it. Chelsea reached forward but then pulled back as if she wasn't supposed to be this close to me. "How's the cat?"

Chelsea smiled, "She's good. Healthy and gets to eat all the chicken she can handle since the cat food plants aren't really operational." She finally reached out to me, touching my shoulder as if to make sure I was real. "She's happy, Daryll."

"How's Kansas City?" I asked. I didn't want to get too sappy. Red and I were sappy the other night, enough to hold me over for a while.

"It's as exciting as any post-apocalyptic city could be. People are there, giving it a sense of normalcy at least," she said. "It's kind of boring, to be honest. But Zach does a good job keeping me in spirits, pretending that everything might be okay once again. He really believes that, you know. He really thinks that this will all end and humanity will return to actual normalcy."

"Forgive me if I'm skeptical," I said.

She shrugged, "I'm not entirely on board with the idea actually happening either. I've been feeling like the contaminated are a new species for us to contend with, a sort of challenger to the human race. Sort of like the competition for food between lions and hyenas."

"This isn't an even battle ground, unfortunately. There's some lions working against lions to help the hyena spread."

Chelsea 'bopped' with her lips, the motion of flicking out the slightly moistened lips to create a small 'bop' sound. She used to do it at school whenever she was bored. I haven't heard it in a long time. "We're actually in a search to find the CRU and learn what they are all about. They attacked us back at Kansas City. Two of our trusted guards were actually plants by the CRU, and they betrayed us to try and cripple our supply chain. A few escaped, one called Marvin was the only name I got."

"Marvin?" I asked. There could be no doubt, I mean there could be some doubt, but probably not. "He's the one who attacked me at a mall a while back. I was supposed to be a meal for one of their lackeys, the first blessing." I began pacing around the room before stopping in front of the bottle and taking another drink. "He was just here, the guys you drove out. Four of them, two guards, Marvin and another person who seemed of rank, Marsha."

"There were more," Chelsea said. "They had contaminated at their rear. I counted two, but it could have been more."

"He said," I continued not acknowledging the fact that Marvin could have killed me at any moment. "He said that they feel, the contaminated. They can communicate with them. I saw a part of the ritual on my way here, the way they can communicate and control the contaminated."

"What do you mean? The contaminated feel?" She asked, turning a pale shade. "The contaminated are alive? They are people inside?"

"I don't know," I said. "But there's something more to them, the contaminated. They're not just the mindless killers we thought they were."

She shook her head, Chelsea's tied ponytail waggled with

her movements. "I'm not buying it. He told you that to win you over. Daryll, you must represent some sort of threat to him and the CRU."

"They listened to him," I said, pouring a bit more scotch in a glass. I took a sip, my body already beginning to feel warm. "He can control the contaminated, and so can others."

Chelsea poured her own, "Maybe so, but that doesn't explain why he singled you out to join them. There is more to this, for a fact."

"I don't think so. It is what it is. In the state of the world, that is how many things are now, Chelsea."

"But they can be better," she said. "Every day is another step in a different direction. Whether it is a better way forward is yet to be seen, but the compass is still pointing."

It was my turn to shake my head, "I don't know, Chels. You haven't seen what I have seen. You haven't experienced what I have had to do just to survive. It isn't a pretty world out there anymore. The shell is still intact, but the turtle is long gone."

"Your metaphors still suck," she smiled. "Let's go to the others. We can talk more later."

Just like that, she was out the door. She still felt like my Chelsea, but there was something different about her. She changed, not much, but enough to feel like she was foreign to me. I wanted to talk about us, but the conversation didn't lead there; she wasn't interested in talking about that topic.

Before I could object, Chelsea took a swig directly from the bottle of blue labeled scotch, corked it, then motioned for me to go with her. I followed with a shrug and held open the door.

"Hey," Chelsea said as we were halfway through the door. "I know you're thinking it, but I'm not avoiding you." Her hand was resting on my shoulder, the touch was all too familiar. "We just have bigger things to get to before we discuss us, ya know?" I nodded, but for some reason it still hurt.

"Sooooooo," Red started. Chelsea's back was turned to us as she engaged in deep conversation with her party. "You two okay?" Red now had her hand on my shoulder, right where Chelsea's had been. All I could do was shrug. "Later, then," Red said. "I think they're coming back with us. Makes sense as they're not really hostile."

The dark skinned leader with the hard crew cut approached. He had a really cool looking rifle in hand. "We would like to team up with you, for the time being," he said. "The name's Adrian."

"Or Serge," Zach called with a smug look.

Adrian gave a half a turn with his rifle in Zach's direction. He then held out his hand, and I took it. Red did the same. "This way," she said.

We reached a street corner with a tall light post. The complex was only a few yards away. "We don't have Mary," I said to Red. "Go take them in. I'll be back shortly with Mary."

"You're not going alone," Red said. "Not after what just happened."

I gave her a look. She thought I might fly away to meet Marvin in Seattle. "I'm not going anywhere other than back here. I'll be fine. I made it hundreds of miles over to here, I can go another few if needed."

"Nonsense," Zach piped up. "I'll join you on your adventure. Let everyone get settled and we can catch up with a horse search."

I sighed, "There's no point in an argument. But you're not riding side saddle."

Zach laughed, "Missed you too."

I walked off without a second glance back. I wasn't bitter at the situation. It was just as if a life I never imagined having again was back. My old life with the people I knew is now the norm. I'd been isolated for so long, then Red came, and now everything is rushing back all at once. It was a lot.

Zach's heavy footsteps sounded not too far behind me. "See you later!" he called to the group then rushed to catch up to me. "Finally, we're away from them."

"What's that supposed to mean?" I asked. "You gonna whack me?"

"Ha! No, no I have no reason to 'hwhack' you," he said with

a north western United States accent.

"Everyone seems to want to talk to me. Do me a favor and keep it less 'deep' than other conversations you can imagine I'm going to have," I said as I bent down to observe Mary's tracks. There really was no reason to crouch in order to examine her hoofprints, but it made me feel like an actual tracker which was pretty cool. "So what is it?"

"Well," he started. Zach kicked loose dusty snow across the street, "I noticed you and that Red girl are pretty close."

"I wouldn't say pretty close, but I get where you're going," I said. "This way. I think Mary is probably by a park not too far from here. There is open grass, and she's a nervous eater. The park is in the direction of the prints, so let's go that way."

We started walking. I always managed to move at a fast pace to the detriment of my company, but Zach was keeping up with ease. A block and a half passed by without a word, that is, until Zach decided to break the silence.

"So, was your talk with Chels productive?" he asked.

I shrugged, "Not particularly. Told her about some things that I'd rather discuss with the group when we get back so that I don't need to repeat myself a third time."

"I don't blame you for that. I was part of firing instruction back in KC. Some people really just don't get how to use a firearm," Zach said. "Just kept repeating it over and over again. Had two guys who were ex-military who helped out. Turns out they were CRU plants."

"CRU made it that deep into Kansas City?" I asked.

He shrugged, "Yeah. They attacked us which is the point of this mission we're on. We found a couple camps on the way here. Denver was going to be our last stop before we returned to report on our findings to the Governor."

"Who's the Governor?" I asked. "Like the president or something?"

Zach shrugged, his far-too-large leather jacket jostling around with his motion. "No clue. Serge met the Governor, but it is extremely rare for another to meet 'em. They feel it keeps the leader out of the public eye so that operations can go smoothly, but it keeps the authoritative figure intact due to the mystery behind them. But with you and Red, we'll have a ton of information to report and discuss a strategy for moving forward."

"You sure will," I replied. The park was up ahead. I attempted a whistle by placing two fingers in my mouth and exhaling with force, but nothing happened. Zach picked me up from there, an ear-deafening shriek echoing off of the Denver building walls. No sounds followed the echos.

"She must be somewhere else," Zach said.

"You're a freakin mystic, aren't you?"

He shook his head, "Not sure how much I missed this side of Daryll." He began to roll a snowball, "Doesn't look like the horse is nearby. Any other thoughts?"

"None involving where Mary would be," I replied a bit more snarky than I meant. "I haven't been in Denver long, so I really don't know where else she could be," I clarified.

"Alright, whether you meant it or not," he started. "I know where this is going. It would be nice if we could talk about it like, you know, like actual people instead of - something else."

"You want to start, or me?" I asked, pretending to look around for Mary. I had come to terms that she wasn't around, but it was a decent distraction.

"I wanted to be you," Zack said. I whipped around a little too quickly, and he jumped. "I've felt compunction in your absence, but I wanted what was best for her. I wanted to be to Chelsea what you were to her. Really, I had no idea what to do or how to comfort her. She was really down for a while in Kansas City. It was really tough, but I did everything I could for her. But the thing is, I didn't only do it for her. I did it for you, Darryll."

There was nothing to say, nothing to speak. Everything I thought prior to this moment was gone. There was nothing left, no hatred, no pity, no anger or jealousy. It just was. All I could do was nod and sparsely shake Zack's hand. I shook it too long, to the point that the moment became awkward and a bit creepy.

"Let's go. Mary isn't around," I said. "It's a shame. She was a good horse. We had a nice couple of days together."

"That's what the cheap ones usually bring to the table," Zack replied. "Too soon?" he asked when I gave him a look.

I smiled, an actual smile for the first time in a long time. "When your only company consists of murderous demon people, a horse, and a fairly aggressive woman, risque jokes really aren't commonplace."

The apartment building was warm when we entered. Red had the fireplace on the first floor roaring with yellow heat licking against the brick. Due to the fire, the windows had to be blocked with curtains, creating eerie shadows dancing on the walls.

"Be gentle with the wood," she said to the group as she brought them glasses of water. "Really isn't much of the clear burning stuff left. Throw in small chips of regular wood to keep the fire going, but don't let it roar for long. Coals will heat us just fine."

"Where's the soupbone?" The pot bellied man called from upstairs.

Red glared up the stairs, "The what?"

"Soupbone," he said.

"Mattieu, this isn't 1912," she replied.

"I need something to stir the soup."

"Top left," she replied with a grumble.

"You guys got soup together in the short time we were out?" I was impressed.

Adrian looked at me, "You'd be amazed at how strong hunger can drive a man."

"I'm familiar with hunger," I said. "I've gone weeks before. Fortunately, a hare was trying for shelter in the same house I was. Cornered the beast. It got a small chunk of me here," I held up my left pinky finger. "But since I ate the thing I figure that bit of finger came back to me."

Red showed up with a glass of scotch for herself and one for me. I had my fill for a while when talking with Chelsea, so I handed it to Zack. He took a sip then gave it back. "That's the good shit!" Red scolded him as he coughed half of it out.

"Well if good tastes like gasoline…" Zack muttered. Red looked like she was about to stoke the fire with Zack.

"Soup's hot," Mattieu called from up the stairs.

"How's the soupbone?" Red said, a slight heaviness in her voice.

The soup was light but refreshing. The broth edged heat into our bones and scraps of meat from dinner last night incorporated nicely, though the substance of the food ended there. In the middle of winter, there really wasn't much available to eat other than stored foods, which at this point were probably on the way out for the most part. Food only stays good for so long.

"So," Adrian said across the table. His bowl was mostly emptied. He brought it up to his lips before he spoke. "How you all know each other?" He began to drink the remainder of the broth. "What's your story?" he asked me as his bowl returned to the table.

I shrugged, "Knew Chelsea from where we grew up. Zack from an online forum and Red here too. That was after the world went to shit, however."

"There's some obvious personal stuff that I'm not going to dive into here between a couple of you," he said. "And to be honest, I'm more concerned with how functional our group will be over the curiosity towards everyone's personal matters." He took another spoon of broth. "Though the curiosity is there."

I shrugged, "What curiosities?" The table was silent, almost as if Zack and Chelsea were shouting at me to shut my mouth. Red nudged her knee against my own. I placed a hand on her knee and gave it a reassuring squeeze.

"What happened?"

"What do you mean?"

"Why aren't you all together?" Adrian asked. "You grew up with Chelsea, clearly have a history. I know she travelled to Kansas City and you've been on the run for a while now. Something had to have happened."

"We just went our own ways," Chelsea chimed in. She sounded too desperate.

I finally took a sip from the scotch Red brought out earlier.

Adrian gave a big toothed smile, "Look. We're eating dinner in a random house with drinks and decent people. This is now the Vegas of the west."

"We were travelling together, Zack, Chelsea, and me," I said. "As I said, we knew Zack from the online forum. He's a bit more tech savvy than us and found our location. Zack managed to track places with power, likely live places on the map. Kansas City was the most probable. We met another from the forum when Kansas City was a mere leap away."

"What'd that person do?" Adrian asked. His full attention was on me now, both elbows pressing hard into the table as he leaned forward.

"Bit me," I replied. "The fucker was a part of the CRU. He wanted to get into Kansas CIty, but I guess that was too tough for someone of his level of contamination. The solution: contaminate as many as possible and hope they made it into the city and create as much havoc as possible." Red glared at me after I told that part.

"I don't know why I'm okay. I don't know why I'm not a changed person, a contaminated. Fact of the matter is that I thought I was dead, or dying to the point where I'd be shot on sight. Then Chelsea and Zack would either be shot on sight or turned back into the wilderness. The only possible way to keep them safe was to stay behind," I said. I took the blue colored bottle of scotch from Red and poured a glass more than half way. Two long gulps later and I was feeling quite warm. "Got over a cold and the rest is history."

Adrian was leaning back against his chair, now resting on two legs. "I might know why, though it's just a theory," he said. "A person who contracts the contamination parasite-virus is almost always healthy. The body has no way to drive it out since the body thinks that it's a healthy helper. The parasite-virus disguises itself as beneficial to the host. If your body is already fighting off some type of disease, it doesn't leave anything for the contamination to cling on to. It's a stealthy bug, not a fighter. Though once it takes hold, it takes everything as its own. You have no chance from then on."

"You think a cold stopped a disease which is threatening the extinction of humanity?" Red asked doubtfully.

"Sure seems like it," Adrian replied. He pulled over the scotch bottle. Red snatched it before he had a chance to pour any.

"This is the good shit," she said. "Darryll and I only, until I figure you out."

"What do you mean?" Adrian asked.

She shrugged, "There's more to you. You're not just the good tough guy hero you're being made out to be. No, the author of this book has something more in store for you."

"Maybe so," he shrugged, standing up from his seat with a gentle nudge of the chair. "May I have some of the 'not so good' shit?"

"What's your story?" Red asked.

Adrian moved to the kitchen and leaned against the counter. "My story?" he started. "I don't know if you're ready for my story."

"If you're planning on fucking us over, I think it's time for your story," Red said. It was my turn to kick her shins.

He shook his head, "No, definitely not. I have no intention of hurting anyone in this room in any way, shape, or form. As of now, my goal is simply to learn more about the CRU. So be at as much ease as you possibly can."

Mattieu stood up and began to clear the dinner plates. "I think that's enough for one day. We're all exhausted." The middle-aged man grouped all of the bowls together and placed them on the side of the sink. "To bed, please. May we have more understanding heads in the morning, no matter how hungover they may be." He placed a lid on the large pot of soup and put it outside to chill.

Everyone stood up from the table and began to go their separate ways. Before joining me in the hall, Red grabbed a bottle of the aforementioned 'not as good' scotch and thrust it into Adrian's chest. "We're not done but a small token of peace can't hurt," she said before turning down the hall.

Because there were more inhabitants than expected and

less comfortable sleeping arrangements, I stayed in Red's queen size bed. We huddled together without even thinking. It almost came naturally, even though we'd only been together for so short a time.

"Sorry," she muttered to me.

"For what?" I asked. The charred scent of scotch was heavy on her breath.

She shook her curled head, "I got a bit defensive back there. I never thought I'd get like that for anyone ever again."

"Does that mean I'm special?" I smirked.

Our eyes met, "You're special alright." She reached up and kissed me. "Thanks - for not leaving me in sight of Chelsea. We're not going to talk about it now, because it isn't a thing. But the time is going to come when you really see her again. And when that happens, I'll understand why you leave me."

"I'm not going anywhere, Red," I replied.

She half laughed, "That's what they all say." Red kissed me again, deeper this time.

Safe sex, guys.

CHAPTER 11 - A PART

A roar, the sound of crashing thunder echoed early in the morning. I slapped the mechanical clock at my side, not realizing that it wouldn't light up. Instead, I rolled over to Red's side to see it was only 3:30 am. Red looked up at me as I leaned over her. She was clearly in no mood to be awake at this hour. Neither was I, but I forced myself up nonetheless.

The monster roared again. At least three of us in the house knew what type of monster made that noise. A contaminated monster was roaming around. I considered them the 'boss' beasts, the final trial when going up against the contaminated.

I was met by Adrian when I reached the hall. He had his rifle in hand and warm hoodie on, hood pulled up over his eyes. He followed me up the stairs, waiting patiently as I put my leather jacket on and tied my good boots.

"That's the way up?" he asked with a harsh whisper. The room was cold, his voice producing a fog. I nodded as I grabbed my own rifle, checked the magazine, loaded a round into the chamber and followed Adrian up.

He left the door at the top of the building open for me. It was pressed back and held open with snow. Heavy flakes cascaded down onto the open roof as the cold wind whipped them in tight squalls. Adrian was at the roof's edge, rifle resting at the farthest point against the concrete barrier. He pushed snow off at either side, piling it a few inches on either side.

Even in the darkness, Adrian's face went pale.

I aimed down my scope, even though it was entirely unnecessary. A line of massive, hulking creatures was walking down the double lane street directly below us. They were flanked on either side by lines of contaminated, each varying in health and overall size. Two by two the boss contaminated moved, each taking up a lane and a half of roadway.

"That doesn't look good," I stated.

He looked at me, "No shit?" The man's eyes turned back quickly. We had to be on full guard. Even talking, while four stories up, was still a risk that we shouldn't be taking.

I poked my head over the edge of the building. The contaminated were continuing their march unhindered. Based on their movements, a human was among the contaminated; probably controlling them - pushing them forward. A dark maroon cloak encased the body, but their arms were waving and flapping around as if it gave them nothing but delectation to be doing their part in the human extinction. All the same delectation it would give me to shoot them somewhere to incapacitate the body.

"We can't do anything up here," Adrian said through the heavy snowfall. "As long as we don't make any excessive noises, our group should be okay."

"Careful how you lump us together," I started before being able to stop myself. "Sorry. I don't mean to start anything now."

"Good. Now isn't the time for this," he replied, going over to the door. A red emergency light guarded by a gate set was lit next to the door. Adrian reached up, pulled out an eight inch hunting knife, and shattered the light bulb with one swift jab. I was concerned for a moment that he may shock himself, though it was more hope than concern - for a moment of course (I don't wish death on him; but seeing him jibble a bit would've been a funny little revenge). (Does that make me evil?).

He pulled the door shut, stopping right before the lock met the casing. The door was then slowly nudged into place. It closed, only making the clicking noises of the gears grinding into place. Adrian also slapped the deadbolt shut behind him.

"They have an army," I said out loud, confident that we were no longer in danger of being heard.

"Who has an army?" Mattieu asked. He appeared from the

bottom of the stairs behind us, climbing them until reaching the kitchen platform. "Don't tell me that's what all the ruckus was about." He moved over to the table and sat down. I didn't see him pour anything earlier, but he had a bottle of bourbon with a black label in hand. Without moving from the table, Mattieu reached over to the stone countertop and retrieved a glass, pouring the bourbon to the halfway mark. "What? Knowing our mindless murdering marauding enemy has an army is certainly worthy of a drink."

"And I thought Zack was a private poet," Adrian said, sitting down next to Mattieu. He poured some of his own. "You know, I never started drinking the hard stuff until after humanity went to shit. Funny how that works. Humanity is in the worst crisis in - well - humanity, and here I am, finding another way to forget it's happening."

Mattieu coughed ever so subtly after taking a pull of bourbon, "It's only wrong if you drink for the wrong reasons."

Adrian scoffed, "What are the right reasons, then?"

"Because it tastes god damn good," Mattieu advised.

Adrian laughed. He took another drink of the bourbon, enthusiastically clashing his glass down against the tabletop. "How screwed do you really think we are?"

"What do you mean?" I asked, joining the alcoholic convention with a glass of my own.

He gave a fake laugh, "You just saw what was out there, right?" I nodded to confirm. "We can't beat that."

I shrugged, "Not with that attitude."

He laughed again. "Really though, the United States army would have trouble going up against that. There were at least forty - that we saw - of those colossal contaminated. And those things don't go down easy to bullets."

"I'm aware," I said.

"That how they got to you?" Adrian asked.

"Sorta," I replied. "One of those things hit us hard on our way to Kansas City."

Adrian nodded, "That's what I was told. Though they left

out the key addition of their friend being bit by a CRU."

"It's kinda suspicious, don't you think?"

He shrugged, "Don't blame you for taking that route. However, I feel like it could have been worth a try to get you into the city."

"And risk them getting thrown out once I was deemed contaminated? No way."

"Now Adrian," Mattieu started.

Adrian laughed as he shook his head, "Don't give me that line 'now I rarely disagree with you," he did his best Mattieu impression.

"You finally caught on?" Mattieu asked with another sip. His cheeks began to turn fifty shades of ruby. "I was only ever pulling your chain, though I rarely do disagree with you, Adrain."

"There you go again!" Adrian roared with laughter. He was feeling it. I hushed him with a finger.

"Boys night?" a voice called from the hallway. Chelsea emerged in loose sweatpants and a zipper down sweatshirt. "No thanks," she said as Adrian offered her the bottle of booze. Instead, she began to heat water on the stove. "I want to wake up without a pounding headache tomorrow. Pretty scary shit outside, huh?"

"You saw?" Adrian asked. I wanted to, but it still felt like something was missing whenever I spoke with Chelsea.

She nodded, "Yeah. That's a lot of bad shit for humanity."

"Language," Adrian said.

"Sorry, mom," Chelsea replied. I felt a wanting lunge when she said that, the reminiscence of what we once had.

"We playing a game," Adrian slurred. His glass had been empty. Without hesitation, it was refilled. "How screwed is humanity?"

"Not at all," Chelsea said. Red was sixty feet away - if that, and all I wanted to do was reach across the table and take Chelsea back. I wanted to reach over to her like I did Red and kiss her. I wanted her to be mine again. Maybe it was the late night drink. Maybe it wasn't. It was probably something that didn't matter now and never would.

I stood up, bid my friends a good-night wave, and returned to my bed. Red stirred as I lay down. I reached over and kissed her on the lips, Red returning the kiss. I fell asleep as soon as my head hit the pillow.

The next morning was quiet. The contaminated army was no longer marching down Denver, and the city was quiet once more. Adrian was up when I started the coffee pot on the stove. I rummaged through Red's stores for breakfast, but before I could get anywhere, she was up and about getting things ready.

Pancakes were served, and about half an hour later, everyone was tucking into them.

"So what's your plan?" I asked. It was directed at the general group, but seeing as Adrian was their unofficial leader, I looked at him as I spoke.

He shrugged, swallowing hard, "Recon is complete for now. We can return to Kansas City and report our findings there to decide humanity's next move."

"That's all?" I asked.

Adrian shrugged, again. Chelsea gave me a glare and Zack looked confused. "You're on the cusp of breaking this thing wide open. The CRU are heading to Seattle, we know this. Maybe it's not their headquarters and maybe it's just another extension to the next lead, but that is certainly more than you have been going off of so far."

"I was actually thinking for us to leave later today," Adrian said. "All of us."

Red scoffed this time, "You think you can order me around? I have made this place my home. Clearing contaminated, gathering food, and surviving all on my own. You can leave all you want, but I'll decide the path which to follow."

"Relax," Adrian replied. "I won't force anyone to do anything."

"Look," I said. "There's something important about this fight that hasn't been addressed yet." Everyone's faces were looking at me, save Chelsea and Red. "The CRU tried recruiting me. Their leader, or one of them, told me that I had what it takes to receive a special ability. He wanted me to be a contaminated leader." The room was dead silent. Zack dropped his fork before picking it up again and dipping pancake in syrup. "He said they feel. The contaminated feel, have emotions and internal thoughts. They are actually living beings, not just the mindless killers we're looking to get out of our way."

"Bullshit," Adrian said. "If you've been avoiding the CRU for this long, Darryl, you are just a thorn in their pompous bitch-ass side they want gone."

I shook my head, "That is irrelevant. Their reasoning for wanting me does not matter. The fact of the matter is, I know where our enemy is going to be and what they are capable of."

"Exactly why you should join us back in Kansas City."

"Exactly why I should keep pushing forward!" I countered. "We are now deep in the enemy's counsel. Red and I have amnesty. We're the plants you need." I felt a nudge on my leg, noting that Red had not agreed to be a spy.

"It's dangerous, the route you want to follow," Mattieu said with calm. He was a man who could ensorcell a room with peace.

"I'm too close," I said, lowering my head. "I'm too close to having an impact for once in my life. There's the opportunity, slapping me in the face; taunting - shouting at me to just try and walk away, yet here I am. It is dangerous," I said, looking directly at Matthieu. "But if I can have an impact on the life of humanity's survival, I'll gladly face that danger."

"Can I please speak with you?" Chelsea asked.

I nodded. We both stood up, after a gentle grab from Red, and moved into the next room over. Chelsea shut the door behind me. "What are you thinking?"

"Exactly what I should be thinking: finding the way for humans to be safe again," I said.

"At the cost of your life?" she replied. "I know it sounds noble and honorable, Darryl, but we can beat this as a team. Returning to Kansas City is just an alternate route to the same destination, don't you see?"

"Yet any delay could ruin this opportunity. Chels," I said,

placing a familiar hand on her shoulder. "The risk is there; I get it. But opportunity is here as well, hitting me repeatedly in the face wanting to be acknowledged. If I don't go - if I don't explore this chance, I'll regret it for the rest of my life."

"And if it goes wrong?" She asked. "Will you regret that?"

"I don't think so."

"Stop doing this for me!" Chelsea said. "I get it. You miss me, you want me back. That's not wrong to feel, Darryl. But we have established a distance between us. What we had is no longer a thing to have anymore." Chelsea approached me, placing a hand on my shoulder. I waited for the other shoulder to be caressed, but it never came.

"I have stuff I need to do, Chelsea," I said. I wanted to - reach forward and kiss her. But that invisible force stopped me, the one where you know Red is right behind you, someone whom nostalgia can't get the better of. All I could do was give her arm a light squeeze. Then I remembered it, the jewel necklace I lifted from the jewelry store back at MA-L. "This is for you," I said. "Whether you wear it or simply throw it away, it is yours. Back," I choked for a second. "Back when I was stuck in Milwaukee, I came across this and thought of you. Please take it."

I couldn't believe at that very moment, I had never taken the damn thing off. Chelsea took it, holding it by the glittering gold chain. She looked back at me, but before I could let my emotions take hold, I left the room.

The kitchen was packed up by the time I returned.

"I'm going to Seattle," I said to the group. Everyone paused what they were doing: Mattieu scrubbing dishes clean, Zack rocking on his chair's back two legs, Red mid-carry to the sink. "Before anyone objects, my actions are my own. Nobody has to follow me. Your mission was to scout up until Denver, and here you are. You can return to Kansas City and decide your next move from there, but that doesn't sit well with me; which is why I will be going to Seattle to find out what our enemy is really up to."

Nobody spoke right away. There really was nothing to say, lest an objection approached. The fact of the matter is that if they never met me here, their mission would have led the group back to their home. I had an opportunity to change my mission, however.

"We're heading out today," Adrian said. "So if you change your mind, join us."

"Thank you," I replied. "I'll consider it in that situation." I had to leave the room after that, retreating back to the bedroom.

"You could have told me what you were planning," Red said in the doorway. She had a loose jacket on along with sweatpants tucked into her boots. "What happens to you matters, and not just to those people in the other room."

"I need to know," I replied. "He said they feel. Marvin has a different, deeper connection to the contaminated." Red's eyes were on me as I spoke, but I couldn't look at her as I spoke. "What it is...does Marvin feel an apparition? Or is it something else entirely? I need to know."

She shook her head, "Even if I asked you not to go?"

"Don't make me choose, please," I said. "Go with them. They seem to be good people who want the best for humanity. They can help you."

Red looked as if she was ready to hit me, "Don't you dare tell me what to do. Don't act like I'm expendable in your life. I killed - to save *you*. Where you go, I go. CRU guaranteed our safety, not just yours. I'm in this with you, Darryl."

"You're not going to like where I go from here. It may scare you."

"I'm ready for that," she slowly walked over to me. "You are the first person I've really felt okay with in a long while. I want you to feel okay too." I went to hug her, but she denied me. "None of the pussy shit right now. Get your things. They're packing up and leaving; so are we."

Before I knew what happened, everyone was outside the apartment complex, bags in hand. Red distributed extra supplies for the other group's journey home. She had some homemade jerky tossed into a baggie for them to take along. Their bottles were stuffed with snow and horses fed with any grain available.

"Be safe," Adrian said. He reached out, and I naturally took his hand. After a quick shake, he retreated. "The enemy isn't as moronic as we once thought. They have a strong army; you've seen that. Be safe."

Zack gave me a bro hug without words. "Thanks," I whispered in his ear as he pulled away.

Mattieu nodded at Red and I. "I expect you to make soup next time we meet," she said. "You bring the soup, I'll bring the soupbone."

"Kids these days," he muttered before breaking out into a full smile and clapping her on the back.

Without a word, Chelsea came over and hugged me. She was wearing the necklace. "You don't have to go," she whispered in my ear. I immediately felt a pang of guilt in my stomach. "Come with us. You've risked enough. Don't succumb to danger anymore."

"You won't like what I'm going to become," I said into her shoulder.

"I still love you."

"I'll always love you."

We finally pulled apart, though the chord was still strung.

Adrian nodded as he leapt onto his horse. He looked as if he was going to offer one to us, though I knew they needed it more. The information carried in their minds was too important to delay.

"You know where to find us," Adrian said as he pulled his horse around. "Don't forget what I told you."

Chelsea was the last to turn. Zack noticed, but wasn't angry. He placed a hand on her shoulder, giving it a light squeeze. I was beginning to tear up, but I wouldn't let it get the best of me. I watched them go, horses moving at a mild trot down the main road until they turned onto the highway and were out of sight.

I heard a familiar growl as our friends left. "Think we can capture this one?" I asked Red. Everything around us was suddenly quieter than I'd remembered.

"Capture it? What for?" she asked.

"Trust me," I said with a sly smirk, though it really should have been far more maniacal. She caught on but didn't object.

The contaminated surfaced. It wasn't entirely healthy. The rib cage was showing as were more of the bones, especially in the shoulder and knees. This was a contaminated, hungry and ready to feed.

"Actually," I said. "We probably don't need to capture it. Just don't obliterate the beast."

"Whatever you say, cap'n," Red said. She smashed a tire iron she was holding against a metallic lamp post to attract the contaminated to our position. It looked over robotically as soon as she had. "Here 'e comes."

I readied my baseball bat. The old one from the previous book you all know and love. The nostalgia was burning inside me as I hope it is you. The contaminated was springing forward as fast as it could, but I was ready.

With a gargle full of excessive logophobia, the monster lunged with a swiping hand and ferocious teeth. Blood infused drool encased its mouth. It leaked red, contaminating the snow with every movement. I ducked low and swung with a steady swipe. It cut directly into the contaminated's thigh, crashing into the flesh and shattering bone. I'd been neglecting my girl. She wasn't as swift as I was used to, being out of practice, and she bounced right off the bone. I was thrown off balance. My face nearly caressed the pavement, but I managed to catch myself at the last moment. My flank was vulnerable.

"Cover your butt!" Red shouted before a whirl of steel echoed across the wind. The contaminated's leg flew off. The kneecap circled through the cold air after being popped out of the beast. It roared in agony as it fell to the hard concrete.

"Hold it down," I commanded when I regained myself. Red leapt onto the contaminated, forcing it down by placing her elbow at the nape of its neck. "I hope there's nothing to this," I said. I reached for Chetty. Her blade rested against the contaminated's neck. It was no longer struggling, instead gasping for breaths lying nearly dead on the ground.

I pulled out a coffee mug from inside my bag and held it

beneath the contaminated's neck. Red pulled up on its greying hair to expose the throat. I cut deep, slicing well into the bone and clean through the flesh. Dark red blood oozed from the incision, cascading with a steady flow into the cup. The liquid climbed higher and higher, nearly gushing over the edge. I pulled it back with a bit dripping over my bare fingers.

"This isn't going to work," Red said. She stood, then reached up and slammed her blade into the back of the twitching contaminated. It went limp as soon as the metal pierced spine. "I mean - that did, but I'm not totally sure about what you're planning on doing."

"Beat it once, I think I can do it again - at least I hope so."

"Is this something that should be done in a church or something?" Red asked.

The cup was already at my lips. The blood was still warm, steaming into my nostrils. The smell wafted around me causing a nausea I had push down, lest I vomit into the blood.

"Too bad this isn't a chalice," I said, delaying the inevitable.

"You can always put it down," Red replied. "You know that I do not agree with this. Marvin wanted to turn you himself, which is sadly the safer route to take."

"I need a surprise for them, Red," I replied. "They probably don't have any idea that I know - roughly - how this is done. We'll finally be one up on the CRU." The cup touched my lips again. It was cold outside. The cup was no longer steaming, allowing me to hold it up without issue.

A second later, I drank. The blood tasted of powerful salt and stinging iron. It ground up my throat. The liquid burned as it went into my stomach as if I was consuming liquid fire. It rushed down, a flush of heat echoing back up bursting out through my ears. I cried out - heavier and stronger than I could have before. My body was shaking and becoming far too hot. I ripped off my jacket and shirt, rolling around in the snow laced pavement. I was writhing in place as the disease consumed me.

Then it stopped. My eyes remained shut as I stood, a wave of dizziness washing over me. I was able to steady myself after a second. My eyes opened.

"Did it work?" Red asked. She was looking from behind her rifle sights as if it would hide her from me. "Do you feel any different?"

"Not entirely," I replied. My voice was different now. Red stammered back a step. "I'm still me, just a lot warmer. My body temperature is skyrocketing." I felt a tingling in my fingertips, then a warping deep within my skull. It felt as if a chill was washing through me, starting deep in the frontal lobe of my brain and coaxing down into a point in my spine. As the feeling ran inside my body, it began to pull in different directions. I could feel the different places it wanted me to go: three points north, six pulls south, a massive wave west. "There," I said, pointing in the direction of the great pull.

"Let's go," Red said.

"It's beautiful, Red," I said as my body became accustomed to the disease. "My vision is sharper, my body feels stronger, and I know where they are. I feel them, Red." A contaminated ran out into the open street. Red readied her rifle, but before she could aim, I was standing in front of her. "These are my brothers," I said. The contaminated grumbled at me, but it wasn't aggressive. It walked over, calmly and without the trademark roar or lashing limbs. Instead, it stood with me at my side.

Red wouldn't take her eyes, or sights, off of it.

The contaminated lowered its head so that the rear of the neck was fully exposed, the spine. Red was taking steps backwards, slowly, but fast enough that I noticed. "I can't half-ass this," I said to her. "We came this far together. If you really want to run, I won't hold it against you."

Her feet stopped. "Sorry. I'm with you all the way."

My jaw gaped, teeth fully exposed to the cold. They crunched down, hard on the contaminated's spine, splitting the flesh and grinding against bone. I felt a wiry substance clinging to my throat. It edged deeper and slid farther down without any effort or force on my part. The substance settled into my stomach. My body shuddered. Each shake providing a wave of energy coursing along my insides. I was stronger, more powerful already. And my enemy was lining up for me to take that ability from them. They were helping me become stronger and there was nothing they could do to stop me.

"We're going, Red," I said after having my fill. "With this, I will be more powerful than they can ever see coming. Our road is set, the pace will fill. Every contaminated en route will be mine. Every enemy we find will be mine. There is nothing they can do to stop me now. I am the greatest."

EPILOGUE

I should be dead again. The reasons that I can continue to move, let alone write this passage, is something out of a fiction novel. My body was on the verge of breaking, yet here I am. My potential is infinite. Nothing is more powerful than I, and if they are - I will take it down and become better.

They made me this way. They created the monster. They spread the monster around to expand and grow. I am growing tenfold. But the biggest mistake my enemy has made is pissing me off.

They made me this way. They wanted this - to join forces, but I've done it on my terms. They don't know it yet, but there is only one future for them: fear. The fear of knowing that they created the monster without limits or control. The fear of not seeing the future. But now, when they look ahead another step, all they will see is me.

Darryl Willows
Memoirs

ABOUT THE AUTHOR

Who Really Cares?

The author is a guy writing stuff and really think's you'll like it. He/she/it likes writing stuff (^^above) and wants to impress his foolish thoughts and ideas upon the masses. Fortunately for the masses, they'll likely never see this stuff.

BOOKS IN THIS SERIES

Contaminated Documents

The contamination started some months ago, nobody knows how or exactly where it started. The pandemic wiped a good chunk of people out. The CRU isn't helping matters either for that....matter. Name's Daryll Willows and I'm on an adventure to find salvation, or humanity, or puns of the two. Join me in my epic quest of stuff that I do to hopefully achieve a resolution or something like that. Idk I'm not a writer. Ask the author more about it I guess.

The Contaminated

The Contaminated 2